As Our Mothers Made Us

Prequel to the *Emily & Hilda* series

BY

JT HINE

https://jthine.com

ISBN: 979-8-9865819-7-2 (print)
ISBN: 979-8-9865819-6-5 (eBook)

Book design: ebooklaunch.com

Editor: Kim Olson

First edition: December 2024

Dedication

To

Ancestors everywhere,

Who planted the seeds

That gave us our roots.

Contents

TITLES BY JT HINE

Fiction

Lockhart

Enemies

Art to Die for

Emily & Hilda

Rule Number One

Emily Is Hard to Kill

The Marsh

Roads to Rome

Black Amazon

As Our Mothers Made Us

Aliya

Non-fiction

I Am Worth It!

Are You Bilingual?

Translator Education in the U.S.A.

Translations

Video Games – a Retrospective by Nicolò Mulas Marcello
& Alberto Bertolazzi

Combat Aircraft by Riccardo Niccoli

Beyond the Age of Oil by Leonardo Maugeri

Schio: Industrial Archeology by Bernadetta Ricci

Man is Different by Don Zeno (with Emily Adkins)

The Fight against Blindness by Luciano Moretti

The Retirement correspondence of Thomas Jefferson

FOREWORD

EMILY. HILDA. KATHERINE. Three women who star in the novels of the *Emily & Hilda* series. The stories in this collection take place before Emily met Hilda on a lonely highway in the middle of Kansas. Some stories reach back centuries and involve their grandmothers and many-times-great grandmothers; others cover the events of their lives that shaped who they are in the novels.

Unlike the novels, these stories were written on deadline. I needed (and still need) a blog post every Saturday afternoon. So, like a preacher who cannot put off writing this week's sermon, I need to write something for my readers. The novel *Emily & Hilda* appeared serially on the blog before I turned it into a book.

For this collection, I have assembled the stories chronologically and edited them to improve the flow and to avoid repeating background that appeared in the previous tale. Where I have mentioned real places and people (e.g., Masconomet and Winthrop in "Kina Saba," and Larry Ford in "The Prom") I have done so only to set my characters in time and space. Everything about these tales is fiction. I hope you enjoy them.

I am open to feedback about this project. Email: jt@jthine.com, or use the contact form on my website, https://jthine.com.

Thank you,

JT Hine

A NOTE ON LANGUAGES

Native languages appearing in this book include Algonquian, Navajo (Diné), Pawtucket, Proto-Algonquian, and Western Abenaki. I make no claim to fluency in any of them. Before the Contact, Pawtucket was a dialect of Western Abenaki as spoken by the Penacook. The Pawtucket in my fictional story incorporated words from other Native languages through proximity and intermarriage over three centuries.

For the convenience of typesetters and ease on the eyes of Anglophone readers, I have used the Norwegian å to represent the Abenaki sound commonly shown as 8, ∞, or "aw". The sound is close in both languages.

Like the final "s" in English, a final "k" indicates a plural form of animate words in Algonquian languages. Thus, *nigå,* elder, and *nigåk,* elders.

I use the word Navajo to indicate the language spoken by the Diné. This clarifies whether I mean the people or their language.

The first time that a non-English word appears, I use italics. If common enough, I switch to normal font after that. The translation should appear close to the italicized word(s) or be inferred from the context.

Kina Saba

"*MALKI!* NO!!" *Kina Saba* (She Sees Tomorrow) lay down by her feverish mate and took him in her arms. "You cannot die on me. I won't allow it!" She ignored his rashes and running sores.

Malki (short for *Maligek,* Strong One) opened his eyes. She could read the pain behind them. And yet he smiled.

"It is time, my love. You will be the Strong One now." He closed his eyes and sighed. "I will love you always, even beyond…"

She wrapped her arms around Malki until she could feel his heart beating against hers. Shrugging off someone's hand on her shoulder, she clung to him as his pulse became slower, then stopped. He began cooling immediately. A chasm opened in her chest.

Kina Saba wailed. She slid off the pallet, kneeled, and keened, long and hard. Each woman around her added her voice.

Malki had led them for five years. Kina Saba had chosen him as her mate three years before his election. They had worked as a team: in council, in the fields, in the woods, and at the hearth. They were the world to each other, equal and supportive in every way.

He was the last man left, of a line of sågamåk descended from the Bear totem. For the third time in a generation, disease had struck Agawam last winter. By the Blueberry Moon (late July) only seven of their band in the Marsh remained. The other sick one, a young woman who had lost her entire family, died the next night.

The six survivors, all Bear women, had not taken ill, even as the fever raged through the village for months. It took them three days to lay out the bodies of those who had died last.

As the ashes cooled on the pyre, they gathered in the woods next to the Marsh. The way the other five looked at her made Kina Saba uncomfortable.

"*Weleniya,*" she said. (Wise One) "You are the eldest, our shaman and *mdålenno.*" (healer) "I would hear your thoughts first."

Weleniya had seen barely thirty harvests herself, but she had five years on Kina Saba, the widow of their sågamå.

"We need to agree on a *saunksqua,*" Weleniya said, "then decide what to do. Whether we stay or go, our band cannot survive with only six women."

"The English are already clearing land north and west of the Marsh," said *Pahtå* (Fast). She had chosen her mate only last summer and buried him four moons ago.

"Malki told me that Masconomet has gone to meet with the English sågamå Winthrop," said Kina Saba. "He plans to give them land for help fighting off the *Kanienkahaka* (Mohawk) and Mi'kmaq raiders."

Weleniya shook her head. "Not good. The English don't understand the land. It will be worse than if the land were to sink under the sea."

"Who should take Malki's place?" asked *Melwa* (Good). "Even with only six, someone needs to make choices and guide the others."

"And deal with the English," the healer added.

They continued to look at Kina Saba.

"What?"

"You were closest to Malki, and you often took his place when he was away," said the healer. "I would have you as saunksqua."

"As would I," said Pahtå and Melwa together.

"Me, too," said *Åkwa* and *Misipisiw* (Bear and Panther). The two best friends had received their coming-of-age names only last summer.

"I think that was the fastest election ever," said Weleniya. "Will you be our saunksqua, Kina Saba?"

Kina Saba stopped breathing. She felt the blood draining from her head and remembered to breathe before she passed out. *This is so sudden. Malki, what have you done?* she thought. Her heart was racing, but she knew the ways to *aquène* (peace) that her mother had taught her. She centered and opened her eyes.

"*Åhå.*" (Yes).

Weleniya rose in a smooth motion, walked to the oversized wigwam, and came out with Malki's walking stick. It was a little heavy, but beautifully carved with the symbols of his office, now Kina Saba's. The wear of generations of sågamåk and saunksquak had given the stick a dark sheen in the light of the fire.

The shaman held the stick in her hands over her head and faced East. She recited the prayer for new life and new beginnings. Turning to the right, she prayed to the South for strength and courage. To the West, she prayed for wisdom and discernment. Finally, she prayed to the North for peace and calm. Then she picked up her own *mdåkwat* (medicine stick). With her head, she bade Kina Saba rise and hold the saunksqua stick and the mdåkwat.

"Lead us, Kina Saba, not as tribes and Europeans do, but as a saunksqua of the *Ninnuok* (the People), a reconciler and peacemaker. Find the path unseen. Discern the fork to take. And leave none behind."

Night had fallen completely by now. Kina Saba held her stick as Weleniya withdrew her hand and her mdåkwat.

"We need to decide whether to leave and where to go. Regardless, it will require preparation and time. Let's start by making a pile of the things of those we leave behind. What we cannot use, we will dispose of if we leave. As you do this, think about places where we could go, and think about why. It will be a very different life out there."

"The English will soon be everywhere," said Pahtå.

"They will indeed. My former band from the west may take us in, but let's continue this conversation in the morning. When the fire is out, get a good night's sleep. Right now, I need to pray. *Walitebokw, nitsakasok.*" (Good night, my sisters)

The meeting broke up. Even as Kina Saba started toward the deeper woods, personal belongings, weapons and tools were coming out of the house. The women stacked them neatly in piles, not by the previous owner, but by category.

Kina Saba reached the clearing that she knew the deer favored in the day. She sat for a while, considering different options. The English were taking over everything that was flat or nearly so, leaving only rocky hills, and land unsuitable for growing food or building a wigwam. They shot their muskets at anyone who strayed onto what they thought was "their" land. Hunting was becoming difficult as the animals moved away from the settled coastal areas into the forests to the west.

On the other hand, the colonists had left pockets of uncleared land, where various bands (not all of them friendly to the Pawtucket) found space to survive. The epidemics had decimated the People, so in fact, they did occupy less space.

The Pawtucket had never considered themselves a tribe, which led to misunderstandings. Their language, a dialect of Western Abenaki, was closer to the language of the Penacook north of the Merrimack River than it was to the language of the tribes around them. Right from the start, Kina Saba could see the likelihood of an Iroquois raiding party simply taking six women as breeding stock or as slaves. Her band was all that remained of the Bear people. *How can we hold together?* she wondered. She missed the French and Dutch traders, who, while somewhat uncouth, at least treated the People fairly, and returned to their cities in the north and the west every winter.

The English colonists seemed determined to make everyone worship their god. This missionary zeal colored all their relations with the local peoples, so it was hard to have a conversation about simple things like living together. If the Europeans were going to take over the land and not share its use as the Creator had intended, Kina Saba could see that her People would need to adapt somehow. She thought up three or four ways of doing that, and a few English settlements where they might do it.

***

In the morning, the women gathered around the fire after breaking their fast. They sat on their heels, with Kina Saba opposite Weleniya, each with her stick of office.

"Last night, I imagined two options," said Kina Saba. "One is to stay here, going out to Agawam (or whatever name the English give it) to trade. In fact, that is easiest, and we don't need to do anything immediately. Maybe we can find husbands among the other bands or even the English. The other is to move to a place with more people, or an English town."

"But won't they make us convert to, what is it, Christianity?" asked Pahtå. "From what I heard, it makes no more sense than their ideas about land and water."

"Malki and I visited the Wamesit two years ago on our way west," said Kina Saba. "Apparently, the English give converts English names and require them to attend their ceremonies once a week – they call it the Day of the Sun – but other than that they all but ignore the People, who remain free to do what they want. My cousin lives near the falls, and he still says the Prayer at Dawn. Among them, the shaman still discerns their real names and conducts coming-of-age ceremonies. They use their *mdålenno* when they get sick; the English physicians would not come to them, anyway."

"Weird."

"Yes." Kina Saba looked around. "Any other ideas – or places?"

"A lot depends on what Masconomet does with the English sågamå," said Weleniya. "From what I understand, Winthrop wants to get rid of the English who have settled west and south of here and keep the land for himself."

"Malki told me about that, too."

"How soon could this happen?" asked Melwa. "Do we have time to walk to the Wamesit, just to check it out?"

"That's an idea. Any thoughts?" Kina Saba asked. They all nodded in agreement. "Good. Let's finish organizing what we want to take and what to leave. We'll go as soon as we can."

***

As the women walked through the woods, Kina Saba motioned Weleniya to walk alongside her.

"I'm concerned about our future as a band," she said.

"As you should, saunksqua." Coming from the shaman, the title still sounded strange to Kina Saba. "What worries you?"

"We have no men. I am sure that we can all find husbands. We're the best of the Bear people: all healthy, good-looking and able to bear children. But I have not been impressed by the men I see around me. I am concerned that they will take us into their tribes and bands, and we will disappear as completely as I see the other Pawtucket vanishing. Between the diseases and the attacks from the Kanienkahaka and the Mi'kmaq, only one in ten of us has survived."

"What do you propose, Kina Saba?"

"I'm not sure. When Malki and I traveled west two years ago, we stayed with some Kanienkahaka, who belong to the Iroquois Federation. Among the Iroquois, the women rule, and one's identity is passed from the mother's totem, not the father's."

"Interesting. That makes more sense, if you ask me. One knows who the mother is for sure, but not always the father."

"I'm still thinking about this, but I am afraid that soon, the six of us could be the last of the Pawtucket. Should we organize ourselves differently going forward, to preserve the Ninnuok?"

"Let's discuss it with the others when we get to Wamesit. We can all think about it for a while."

***

Wamesit was not a town. Like Agawam, Pawtucket and other names, Wamesit indicated the people as well as the area where they lived. The disorganized collection of wigwams and two longhouses that served as winter quarters for a Pawtucket band contained several families of Wamesit.

The six women set up a wigwam in the woods out of sight of the others, but close enough to participate in the village life. They traded the excess dried fish they had brought for various necessities, so they did not have to rely right away on the wampum they had secreted in their clothes and among their possessions. Living in the Marsh had blessed them with an abundance of the shellfish that the Pawtucket fashioned into the currency of the region.

The week after they arrived, Kina Saba was approached by a man in dirty English clothing. He spoke Pawtucket, and he did not look European. He had waited on the other side of the street, as if deciding whether to cross or not. She did not like the way he looked at her. She had seen that look on European men, and a few Native men before Malki would call them on it by clearing his throat.

"You seem to be the leader of the six women who arrived last week," he said. "I am John Brown."

"Kina Saba of the Bear people. You have an English name."

"I am Christian. They gave me John as a name. We came from Agawam on the Merrimack River."

"I have cousins there."

"Not anymore. We are the only survivors." He waved an arm at the village. The motion released body odor, but Kina Saba held her breath discreetly.

"I am sorry. We have lost everyone, too."

"I guess you are not Christian."

"No. How does that work?"

Brown explained the daily church school that met during the week, and the requirement to attend services on Sunday. They could learn English and how to read and write.

"That seems like a good thing, John. Thank you."

That evening, the six Pawtucket agreed that learning English and writing would be useful regardless of what the future held. They showed up every day together and began attending services the following Sunday. The four older women already spoke English (and some Dutch and French), and they helped Misipisiw and Åkwa learn quickly. The writing was more fun than anything else, so by the time the leaves began to turn, all six women were functionally literate.

They kept to themselves out of sight in the woods, near a stream that fed into the Merrimack. They took jobs as servants in English homes nearby. The men they met did not attract any of them.

"They have no responsibilities," observed Weleniya one evening. "They can't farm or hunt here, and the family men seem to have taken the jobs working for the English on their farms. It must be depressing."

"Maybe that is why many of them drink that awful stuff the English make."

Melwa put another stick on the fire. "Maybe we should move again – or go home. We can meet men in Agawam just as easily as here, without having to listen to that preacher every week."

***

Kina Saba was walking home from the Lowell farm in the evening when she heard a scream in the woods to her right. It sounded like Åkwa. Kina Saba turned into the brush and ran as quietly as she could toward the noise. She heard crashing noises and shouts from men.

She slowed at the edge of a clearing and saw two men pulling on Åkwa, one on either arm. One was John Brown. The girl's face was ashen, and her eyes were wide with panic. Kina Saba froze for only a second, then reached for a rock at her feet.

"Let her go!" She threw the rock at Brown. It hit him in the head. He released his grip, but did not fall.

"You bitch!" he growled and staggered toward Kina Saba. *He must be drunk,* she thought. *That happens with too much of that English drink.*

Before she could draw the knife she always carried, he leaped at her, grabbing her arms. His momentum drove her backward, and he emitted a powerful stench as they fell. The ground was soft, or she would have passed out when she hit her head.

He was heavy, and hot. He kept his hands on her elbows, pinning her to the ground. She felt a surge of bile as she struggled, less to push him off than to keep her focus. She tried to recall what she and Malki had drilled when she was learning to fight and defend herself.

He was pushing her down, bruising her mons pubis with his bulk. She had her legs together but felt him trying to get his knees between her legs. She lifted a shoulder to meet his next push and got her knee up to his crotch. His hands released slightly, and she immediately reached down and squeezed his testicles with her left hand.

He screamed, opening space between them. With her right hand, she drew her knife. She pushed up with her legs, then drove the knife into his chest exactly where Malki had taught her. She rolled him off herself as he died, then stood.

The other man was humping on top of Åkwa, oblivious to his friend's demise behind her. Kina Saba picked up the stone again and brought it down hard on the back of his head. She heard a satisfying crack as his skull fractured. She pushed him over.

Åkwa was still screaming but stopped abruptly when the weight above her vanished. She looked up with tear-filled eyes in her flushed face. Kina Saba knelt by her. Her skirt was pulled up, but Kina Saba saw no blood on her.

"Did he–?"

"I–, I don't think so."

Kina Saba pulled her up and hugged her.

"I think we have our plans made for us. Let's get back to the others."

Walking with a full moon, the six women were more than twenty miles away by the next morning when they arrived at the village of Agawam. Kina Saba and Weleniya reported the situation to Masconomet, who gave his blessing to their returning to their wigwam in the Marsh.

He also alerted his people to be on the lookout for any Wamesit coming from the west, but no one ever followed the women.

***

In the years that followed, Kina Saba and her band enlarged and strengthened the wigwam, built storage huts for winter food, fished, and traded. By 1638, Masconomet had sold all the land around the Marsh to Winthrop's son. The English planted farms around the edge of the Marsh, but no one seemed interested in what was happening in the Marsh itself.

The women mingled with the survivors of other bands, and all found husbands well before King Philip's War, which the descendants of Masconomet wisely stayed out of. Kina Saba herself married a Massasoit from the south, and the couple took the English-looking surname Massey.

By the dawn of the 18th Century, no one remembered them, and Kina Saba's daughter, now saunksqua herself, continued the band as her mother had set it up with Weleniya and the others. Their English neighbors paid them no mind.

The women were careful in their selection of mates, and they made sure that the men were willing to live and work as equal partners. They also consulted with their Pawtucket sisters before proposing. Their children were full members of the band.

Some of the men were from different totems, and some were European. Soon the sisterhood of Pawtucket survivors and their descendants disappeared into the general population, with their men, their sons, and their daughters.

Being literate, the saunksqua or sågamå of each generation meticulously recorded all the births, marriages, and deaths of the little band. They had their children christened in local churches and sent them to local schools, but they also raised them in their heritage. Kina Saba and her successors could see that the patriarchal hierarchy imposed by the English and American governments would consign their children to a complete loss of their heritage. The records remained in the Marsh, carefully handed down from one sågamå or saunksqua to the next.

In the middle of the 19th Century, when the Commonwealth of Massachusetts was busy incorporating towns and responding to the realities of the Industrial Revolution, Mildred Massey, who lived in the Marsh, had the ownership of the house and the Marsh recorded in Essex County in her name, noting that Winthrop's original claim had not specifically named the Marsh as part of Agawam, by which the original English settlers had meant only the named localities of the area, where they intended to establish farms. This would prove crucial a century and a half later when the state needed to preserve the barrier islands of the northeast coast.

NOT OUR WAR

WLIWELJI (Gentle Hands) ran through the woods silently, careful not to slip on the thick carpet of wet leaves. Her breath steamed and her heart pounded, not from the running, but from fear. The body had risen from the water when it caught on the net she was using. She saw the half-dozen wigwams that comprised her village, and her grandmother, stirring something over the communal fire.

At the sight of the tall, broad-shouldered woman, Wliweji felt relief flow over her. The older woman had that effect on everyone in the village.

"Nigå!" Wliweji cried. "There is a dead man in the creek!" A nigå is an elder, and includes grandmothers, uncles, aunts and others worthy of respect for their age.

Mliki (Strong One) straightened up. She put a hand on the girl's shoulder to calm her, as Wliweji's mother came from their wigwam. *Kzihla* (She Runs Fast) crouched by her daughter.

"What did he look like?"

"Swollen, like a dead deer. He had a big hole in his chest."

"Clothing?"

"A red wool coat, and long black boots."

Kzihla looked up at Mliki. "British soldier, Nigå."

"This is not good," said the elder. She reached inside the wigwam for her walking stick. "Let's go look. Wliweji, lead us."

The three women returned to the inlet where the girl usually fished. The dead man was an officer of some kind, which they deduced from the gorget around his neck.

"Less than two days," said the nigå. "He doesn't stink yet."

"Should we bury him or take him away?" asked Kzihla.

"Whatever, we must do it quickly, before he is missed or pollutes the creek." Mliki put a hand on Wliweji's shoulder. "Run to the village. Find the mdålenno and bring her back with the big spade we keep in my wigwam."

While the girl ran, the two women pulled the dead officer ashore. Fortunately, he had been a slight man, perhaps less than eighteen harvests and weighing not much more than they. They made a stretcher, because a travois would leave obvious tracks. The healer arrived with Wliweji and the spade.

The little group carried the corpse to the northwestern edge of the Marsh, where the river flowed between their woods and the farms east of the English town of Rowley. The colonists rarely came into the woods, but if they came across the grave so close to the town, they should not have reason to venture into the forest looking for his killer.

"What about his knife?" asked Wliweji.

"It would be nice to have a fine blade like that, but we cannot afford to have the Europeans discover us with it."

"I understand, Nigå."

"But you gave me an idea." Mliki removed the knife and its holster and flung them into the deep channel in the river. "Should anyone discover the body, they should not have to wonder why it was not stripped of its weapons."

***

That night, Mliki called a meeting of the Pawtucket band. About thirty who had come of age gathered around the fire, some finishing the last of their evening meal. They sat quietly, centering their spirits and banishing the distractions of the day.

Mliki had been elected saunksqua to succeed her mate, who had been sågamå for ten years when he was killed. Twenty harvests had passed since he had been caught in the wrong place at the wrong time: walking home from a day of trading, when a bar fight spilled out of the pub in Rowley. She mourned him still in her way, taking deep satisfaction in her daughter and granddaughter, who reminded her of him in so many ways.

From six women of the Bear totem, who had hidden in the Marsh after the last epidemic in 1635, the remnant had grown to a dozen families. The English colonists had little interest in the Marsh, it being unsuitable for their large farms. The woods extended to the water on all sides, effectively hiding the Pawtucket from the Europeans using the rivers and creeks for their boats. Natives fishing in the Marsh were a common sight, and the English did not notice or care where they went at night.

It was a safe, quiet world. They had meat from deer and small animals, abundant fish to eat and to dry for trading, and a cornucopia of different shellfish. The shells were used to fill in watery places and to make wampum, the universal currency of the Algonquian tribes. The small band had built bigger, stronger wigwams, so that they could winter over in the Marsh instead of migrating inland.

Mliki rose and brought her walking stick to the circle. She raised it to the west and prayed for wisdom and discernment. Then, she sat cross-legged and addressed the band.

"We have a problem, not of our making. We know that the colonists are unhappy with their king, and we have heard them talking of rebelling against him." She looked at her granddaughter. "Tell them, Wliweji."

"I snagged a dead Englishman in my net today." She paused. Mliki nodded. "An English officer."

"That is serious," said her great uncle. "The rebellion is spilling into the open."

"I'm afraid it is," said Mliki. "The English tried to enlist the tribes around us when they fought the French, and they would expect us to fight with them now."

"But who is their enemy?" asked an old man, who had fought as a teenager against the French. "They are all English as far as I can tell."

"I have heard people in town talking about Americans," said a woman who often who carried fish into Ipswich to trade. "America is what they call our land."

"The English sågamå in Naumkeag has sent for more soldiers from the west," said a man recently returned from a trading trip to Salem. "Soon there may be bloodshed among these English."

"We need to agree on our part in this conflict," said the saunksqua. "Do we side with the English or the so-called Americans? Do we move? Do we stay out of it, if possible?"

Each question had as much going for it as any other. The Penacook to the north were being courted by both sides. Many tribes had migrated west, which put them in conflict with the *Kanienkahaka* (Mohawk) of the Iroquois Federation.

"Saunksqua?" asked Wliweji.

"Yes, *Noses*." My grandchild.

"Do you remember King Philip's War?"

Mliki laughed. "Goodness, no, but my grandmother Kina Saba was our saunksqua then. Why?"

"Didn't we stay out of that one?"

"You're right. We did. Of course, we were still hiding from everyone at that point. I think we had only four families at the time."

"I have only seen fourteen harvests, but it seems to me that this is not our war."

Wliweji shivered as the silence lingered. She felt embarrassed and ashamed as the gazes of her elders bored into her. Most had a distant look, as if they were thinking. Others seemed surprised. Her mother was smiling.

Mliki reached for her walking stick and brought it up. The wood shone in the firelight, as much from polishing as from the wear of generations of sågamå and saunksqua who had held it.

"It is an omen that Wliweji is sitting in the west. What say you all?"

"*Åhå, wawådåzo*," they answered together. Yes, she is wise.

"From tomorrow, we will restrict our trading to bare necessities and send out only one or two at a time. Dry our excess meat and fish for storage, and gather firewood to season well so it will not smoke."

By the time the Commonwealth of Massachusetts joined the new United States of America, no one remembered that they used to see "Indians" in the Marsh…

SHREDDED!

KATHERINE CLIMBED THE FIRE ROAD, reveling in the feeling of her heart pumping and her legs moving smoothly. The wind carried the scent of pine and wood smoke as it tugged wisps of her auburn hair loose from under the helmet.

She remembered the day she stood by the trail and watched the racers flying down the gullies. At eleven, she had already been riding for seven years, and her father had bought her a new bike when they arrived in San Anselmo. The memory of that race still thrilled her.

She did not know at the time that she was watching the very last running of the Repack Downhill, an iconic chapter in the development of mountain bike racing. By the time she finished sixth grade, the racers had grown into their different interests: bike shop owners, frame builders, mechanics, and organizers. MTB racing was here to stay, and from its birthplace in Marin County, it spread like wildfire. Katherine and her classmates rode at the center of that conflagration.

Her coach, Jeb Mandrake, had been part of the Larkspur Canyon Gang after the founding members recruited him. Now he managed a bike shop in San Anselmo but also coached a mountain bike team of

Drake High School students. If efforts to create a high-school level MTB organization were successful, Drake would have a ready-made varsity, but by then, Katherine would be gone. She had already made her mark when Jeb invited her to join the team.

"I don't care if she's a girl," he had told her parents. "She's faster and more skilled than the boys. Brawn won't work in this sport."

Jeb was waiting at the trailhead. They chatted until the others arrived. Katherine was the only one who rode to the trailhead. As the others unloaded their bikes from cars and pickup trucks, she dove into the trees and brush, then climbed to the top.

When the coach and the five boys caught up with her, Katherine was racing back and forth across the clearing, seeing how long she could maintain a wheelie (riding only on her back wheel). Mostly, she was trying not to cool off too much waiting for the others. She spun around on an outbound leg and came to a two-wheel stop by the others.

"Impressive, Katherine," said Jeb. "Gather around everyone." Phil Yancey, Katherine's classmate at Drake High School, smiled; he had seen her do that stunt often enough. The four younger boys stared in awe at the tall senior girl, until the coach waved his hand in front of their faces.

"You've all ridden the trail to Lagunitas enough. Most of the races around here are downhills, but the Lagunitas Challenge is a super-D. Today, we start practicing the mass start. Any questions?"

"Is it true that the Challenge has more than a hundred riders registered already?" asked Phil.

"I don't know about that," said Jeb. "Two days ago, only three dozen had completed registration, but there is still a month to go. I'll tell you this, though. The competition will be tough. Teams are coming from at least Colorado, Utah, and Nevada. You'll be the only high-school team there."

"Why?" Robert, a high school sophomore, asked.

"Because the Drake team is unofficial. Officially, you're an under-twenty-three team sponsored by the bike shop in San Anselmo." Jeb clapped his hands together and pointed to where they should lay down their bikes, and then where to stand for the start.

In the week before the Lagunitas Challenge, the out-of-state teams trickled into Marin County. The local teams, like Jeb's U-23 team from Drake High School, had to wait for chances to practice their mass start for the event. The skill with which the Drake students ran to their bikes and flew down the trail caught the attention of the other teams.

One of the organizers approached Jeb one day. Jethro Smith (call me "Jet") had arranged for television coverage, and financed a team from Park City, Utah.

"Who is the rider with a ponytail on your team?" He asked Jeb.

"Katherine Millbank."

"But she's a girl."

"As a matter of fact, she is. Is that a problem?"

"We don't have girls in these events."

"You haven't banned them."

The impresario from Utah was clearly uncomfortable. "I need to speak with the others."

"It's rather late to change the rules or create one that excludes our best rider."

"We'll see." He turned and walked away.

***

"Hey, Millbank!" Katherine recognized the nasal voice. She let go of the trigger and hung the hose on the top tube of her half-rinsed bicycle. Her gorge rose, but she swallowed hard and breathed slowly to stay calm.

"Hello, Ricky. I see Kentfield College has a team in the Challenge." Ricky Anderson had been a year ahead of her at Drake High School. Now he attended the local community college. She did not like being civil to him but forced herself anyway.

The beating under the bleachers of the football stadium still brought her nightmares. Ricky had fled when the police showed up. The police had arrested the two boys that she had decked, after the paramedics carried them away. The officers chose not to go after Ricky. Katherine's cracked rib healed in a couple of weeks. The memory, while less painful, burned in her gut two years later, as much because Ricky got away after instigating the attack as for the suspension she pulled for fighting back.

"Yeah. What are you doing here?" He waved at the pockets of riders rinsing their bikes or loading them into cars and trucks to drive away.

"Same as you. We just had a practice run." Seeing him come closer, she put her bicycle between them and picked up the hose. "Gotta finish rinsing my bike so someone else can use the hose."

"You can't ride the Lagunitas. You're a girl."

"Oh, get over it, Ricky. Have you ever beat me in a race?" She met his gaze, holding the hose ready to soak him. "Now back off and go somewhere else. I put up with enough from you before."

Ricky took a step. She raised the hose. He stopped, clenching his fists. Then he turned sharply and walked to a muddy pickup truck across the parking lot. He lifted the bicycle leaning against it into the bed, got in, and drove away.

Katherine let out her breath, surprised that she had been holding it so long.

***

At the edge of the parking lot off Sir Francis Drake Boulevard in Lagunitas, a heated argument was in progress. Jethro Smith and the coaches from Utah and Nevada on one side; Jeb and the coaches from Marin County on the other. The coaches from Washington, Oregon and Colorado were watching silently.

"So what if she's a girl?" said Jeb. "What part of this sport requires a dick?" He clenched his fists and stepped closer to the businessman from Utah. The other coaches took in a sharp breath and froze.

"Easy, Jeb." Marty, a bike shop owner from Fairfax, put a hand on his friend's arm. Jeb shook it off.

"I've been racing mountain bikes from the start." He pointed at the impresario. "Where were you when we rode the Repack Downhill? Have you ever shredded a trail? We know this sport. It calls for the strength of a gymnast and the nimbleness of an acrobat. Millbank's got those in spades."

"But she could be hurt," said Jethro.

"Of course she could be hurt! So could the others. I've seen her finish a downhill with a dislocated shoulder and blood running down her arms." He looked at the other coaches from Marin County. "Help me out here, guys. You've seen her race. She puts the men to shame – and puts on a better show than any of them."

Marty said, "He's got a point. She really does drive the crowd wild." He turned to Smith. "You're in this for the advertising and the money. You'll get more ROI on Millbank than any of the other riders." (Return On Investment) "Stop fighting this."

The atmosphere settled as the men considered the aspects of the case. After a while, Smith sighed and extended his hand to Jeb with a smile.

"Good luck, coach."

Jeb shook his hand and grinned. "Thanks, Jet. By the way, don't let her hear you talk about the weaker sex. You could end up with a split lip."

The Marin coaches snickered at that.

***

The butterflies made Katherine clench her teeth in a mighty effort to ignore them. Her parents had driven her to the trailhead, because they wanted to watch the finish. The parking lot was packed, with cars and pickup trucks parked on the side for a half-mile in either direction.

She hugged her parents, gave her bike another once-over, then rode to the edge of the parking lot. The butterflies settled when she felt the shade of the trees over her and the familiar roll of the rising trail.

The clearing at the top was littered with bikes and riders. Each team had gathered away from the starting "line", a yellow tape among the trees across from the top of the trail. The bikes of the next team to take off were lying near the trail, their riders lined up with a hand on the tape.

Two officials stood by the team. One had a whistle, the other held a bag phone, talking to the officials at the finish line, so they could start their clocks at the same time. A third official stood by the bikes.

The team from Kentfield College was holding the tape, trying to lean toward their bikes. The whistle blew. The men dashed across the clearing. They picked up their bicycles and started down the trail. Katherine noticed that Ricky Anderson was second or third down the hill. Two riders fell trying to jump on their bikes, so they were the last out of sight.

After three teams had started down the trail, the Drake students (Anselmo Aces, officially) rolled their bikes to the to the top of the trail, laid them down, then walked to the tape. The bikes were well spread out, because there were only six riders on the team.

Katherine squinted at her bike, took a deep breath, and rolled her shoulders. She felt her focus grow. Her fears and worries, along with everything else that did not have to do with the race, melted away. She was five yards from the tape when the sound of the whistle died. She pulled her bicycle up by the handlebars, pushed it away from her toward the trail and swung with her arms onto the saddle as the bike started down the trail. It was a maneuver that put her halfway to the first curve before the second rider started down the trail.

The trail was so familiar that she could notice how much the first three teams had shredded it ahead of her. She focused on spotting the differences as she flew from one curve to the next, jumping new gullies, and using new gouges in the trail to pitch herself a little higher on her jumps.

Katherine was alone with the trail and the forest, one with the flashing sunlight and the passing shadows. There was nothing in her world but the next curve, the next obstacle, and – there – the finish line. She was aware of the crowd, the officials, the cars, but did not look at them. She saw only the line of yellow and black daring her to break it with her handlebars or chest.

She flew through the tape and found herself in the air, flying high away from her bicycle.

As her body twisted, she looked back. Her bicycle was cartwheeling in a straight line, something in its front wheel. The broken finish tape flapped from its headset.

Then, darkness…

***

Time passed. Or did it? In the blackness, Katherine heard nothing, smelled nothing, felt nothing. She could not even tell if she was lying down, standing, or falling.

At some point, she became aware. Of what, she did not know, but maybe she was not dead. The awareness grew, until she realized that she was lying on her back. She heard a distant noise and understood where her ears were. Feeling returned, at first as a tingle, then building, until she recognized pain. She almost smelled disinfectant and fear before the pain grew enough to displace her other senses.

Carefully, she inventoried her parts as she felt them. First, the ones that hurt the most: arms, head, leg, back. Slowly, she mustered the rest: stomach, intestines, heart, lungs, fingers, feet.

She found her eyelids. Light pressed on them. She saw the blood vessels in them. She had never noticed those before. They gave her world a redness in the black all around her. She considered opening her eyes (*Is that something I can do?*). In her hesitation, she wondered if that would hurt more or less than everything else.

She lifted her eyelids.

The bright light stabbed the back of her eyes into her brain, drowning for a moment the other pain radiating throughout her body. She slammed her eyelids shut and squeezed them hard.

The light receded.

"Hello, Katherine, you can open your eyes now."

She did.

"Daddy."

"Yes, dear. Sorry I could not get up to block the light in time."

"Mommy?"

"She's coming. Now that you have woken up, I know you'll be okay. We can talk about it later."

"Thank you." She slept…

***

Fire. Trembling, twisting, all-consuming fire. Katherine snapped awake, shaking from the torture. Her first reaction, to sit up, nearly made her pass out when her contracting muscles added their stabbing knives to the flames.

She did manage to turn her head before opening her eyes, so the overhead lamp did not blind her.

Her mother sat on the visitor's couch, her head bent in sleep. Louise Millbank's auburn hair, still thick and shiny, fell to either side of her head, covering her broad shoulders. Her head and shoulders rose and fell gracefully with her breath. Just in time, Katherine suppressed the urge to speak and reached out for the feeling that rose in her as she watched this woman who had obviously kept vigil in this hospital room past the point of exhaustion. With that feeling came the realization that *yes, I will be alright.*

The pain finally won out. She could not ignore it. "Mommy?"

Louise snapped back, hair flying back behind her head, eyes wide and mouth open. She leaped to her feet and crossed the room.

She reached out, then stopped short of touching her quivering daughter.

"You're awake."

"Yes, Mom. It hurts so much. Everywhere."

Louise picked up the call button and pressed it. "Let's get the nurse in here."

The nurse arrived immediately. By then, Katherine was taking slow, labored breaths, trying not to move, which only made the pain worse. The nurse opened the valve slightly on one of the bags attached to the needle in her arm.

"You should feel better soon – at least be able to stand it," she said. "We couldn't give you more painkiller until we had you awake."

Whatever it was felt like a warm river going into Katherine's arm, spreading to the rest of her body. She focused on the nurse's badge: Dawn Meadows, R.N.

"Thank you." She looked at her mother. "What happened?"

"A stick in your front wheel threw you over your handlebars. You crashed into a tree at the end of the trail." She put her hand on Katherine's arm, gently. "Let me call your father."

"Doctor Millbank is on his way," Dawn said.

"Is this San Rafael?"

"Yes, it is. Your father came out of surgery an hour ago. He has been keeping us informed where he is."

"How long have I been out?"

"Two weeks. Your father and the attending physician can answer your questions."

Martin Millbank pushed through the door followed by a younger doctor. Katherine's father paused to hug his wife, then joined the other doctor at the bedside.

"Hello, Katherine. You probably don't feel like it, but you look a lot better." He indicated the other man. "This is Roger Shen. He's an orthopedic surgeon, and the lead doctor on the team that put you back together."

"What happened to me, Daddy? It hurts everywhere."

"It should. Fractured skull, even with the helmet. Whiplash. Concussion. Both arms broken. Compound fracture of your left tibia, three broken ribs and two cracked vertebrae. Doctor Shen's team put it all back, but we had to wait for you to come out of the coma to see what other damage there is.

"When you recognized me last week, I knew you could recover."

Doctor Shen said, "We have more tests to conduct, but your body does seem to be healing very fast." He looked at the wall clock behind her, checked the figures on the monitor, then examined her dramatic bruises. "That's enough excitement for today. We'll be back to run you through x-rays, CAT scans, and other tests. Right now, just rest."

"Thank you, Doctor." Katherine's eyelids felt heavy.

Martin and Louise took turns leaning over Katherine and kissing her forehead, almost the only patch of skin on her body that was not some brilliant color.

"One of us will be here all the time," her father said. "I'm going to the cafeteria. I'll bring my lunch back with me."

Katherine smiled and closed her eyes. The morphine took her back to sleep.

***

As the first snows covered the mountains of Marin County, the Millbanks celebrated Thanksgiving on cafeteria trays, though Martin and Louise brought the meal in a large picnic basket from home. There was much to be thankful for as they gathered around Katherine's hospital bed.

"Your mother and I knew that you healed quickly," said Martin, "but those were the scrapes and cuts of childhood. The staff here is amazed at how fast your bones are knitting."

"The nurses panic when they see me going to the bathroom by myself, but if I use the walker until I'm out of sight, they don't hover over me."

"And the bathroom?"

"With the handicap bars, I'm fine. I just let myself down and get up slowly."

"I know you made a deal with Roger not to take the painkillers unless you needed them. How has the pain been?"

"Nothing acute for the last week. If I don't try to move fast, it's just the usual background pain of things healing. No worse than the broken ribs I had two years ago."

"Have you been getting in and out of bed by yourself? You gave me a start last Friday when you did that."

"Yes, although I promised the nurses that I would call them so they could watch.

"I can also stand up straight and walk normally, but don't tell anyone. I have only crossed the room and back so far."

"I'm proud of you, darling, but don't push yourself. Rehab will push you enough."

"How much longer will she be here, Martin?" asked her mother.

"She'll need a wheelchair and a walker, but she could come home by Christmas. I'll talk to Roger about it." He turned to his daughter. "Would you like that?"

"Yes. Doctor Shen said that I would start rehab on Monday. Would I keep coming here after I'm discharged?"

"I'll check on that, too. If you can go home by Christmas, you should be able to go back to school in January with a cane or crutches."

Katherine tilted her head to the long, tall table between her bed and the window. It was covered with books and papers. Her parents had shuffled her assignments back and forth so that she could keep up with her schoolwork.

"There's my homework for this weekend. Would you drop it off, please?"

The family ate in silence for a while. Katherine noticed that her father's gaze was off in the distance.

"Dad, is something wrong?"

"Maybe. I'm still trying to make sense of it." He looked at Louise then back to Katherine. "The police called this morning. The crash was not an accident. Someone in the crowd shoved that stick into your wheel."

Katherine bit down on her turkey so hard that it made the healing fracture in her skull ache. She gasped and paused to catch her breath. She exchanged a stunned glance with her mother.

"Sabotage?"

"Apparently. The television footage of you coming through the tape showed an arm sticking out of the crowd, pushing the stick at your wheel, but the person at the other end of the arm was hidden by the bystanders."

"The crowd was right up to the trail, I remember. I was afraid that I might hit someone when I saw the final stretch."

"How did they get away?" asked Louise.

"Quickly, I would say. In the shock of Katherine's dramatic air show, he – if it *was* a he – only needed to turn and walk away."

"My God, who would do such a thing?" Louise's face was pale, her eyes still wide in shock.

They looked at each other without speaking. Katherine sighed first.

"I can think of at least six or seven boys who would want to do this. And two or three of them would be mean enough to try it."

"So many?" asked her father. "There were only three in that fight that got you suspended."

"I didn't bring the others home."

Louise put her tray on the coffee table. "Why didn't you tell us?"

"Because I took care of it."

"Let me guess," said Martin. "You beat up the bullies?" Katherine nodded. "That's not a good way to solve problems like this, you know."

"Dad, I started dealing with bullies in seventh grade. Since then, no one has picked on me. But I don't let them pick on others, either."

Her father looked intensely at her while he took a sip of his juice.

"The fight wasn't bullying, was it?"

"No. Ricky Anderson and his friends thought they would teach me a lesson."

"Why?"

"Because they can't stand having a girl do anything better than they. In this case, race bikes. But I also took a lot of crap after winning the track events that spring."

"Why would that bother them?" Louise asked. Katherine tilted her head to her father.

"Someone noticed your times," said Martin. "Ricky Anderson and his friends ran track?"

"Ricky did. The other two played football. They were just thugs." She paused. "I guess we'll never know, but those three are the ones I would expect to pull something like this. The boys I've either shown up or beat up would want to do that, but the bullies wouldn't have the guts."

Martin folded his arms and leaned back while he considered his daughter.

"Katherine, do you need anger management therapy?" He grinned. She relaxed and smiled back.

"No, Dad. I don't get angry. Really. Boys like that annoy me, but I ignore them. And I ignore the bullies unless they pick on someone who can't handle them."

"Where did you learn this? We did not teach you to fight."

"Except that once, it was never a fight. All it took was for me to confront the bully to make him stop. If he tried anything, I usually disabled him and warned him off." Martin raised an eyebrow and rolled his hand. "Remember Mr. Whelan?"

"The wrestling coach."

"After the first time I was picked on in seventh grade, I read up on bullies a little in the library. I knew Mr. Whelan had been a Green Beret – all the girls in middle and high school had a crush on him. I explained the problem and asked him to show me a few defensive moves to discourage bullies. He was happy to help. After I put down the second bully, the word got out to leave me alone. After that, I studied unarmed combat books and tried new moves until I felt confident enough to defend myself or anyone else."

For about five minutes, no one spoke, while they ate their pumpkin pie, and her parents considered this revelation about their daughter.

"You never were a shrinking violet," said her father, "but I had no idea what a tomboy you are."

"Oh, come on, Dad. I still like a pretty dress. I happen to like sports, and I won't stand for someone telling me I can't do something because I'm a girl."

"You won't get any argument from us." He smiled at his wife. "Right, dear?"

"Just how much fighting have you been doing?" Louise asked.

"I don't know. It seems to take a couple of weeks at the start of every school year to establish boundaries with the boys. After that, I only need to threaten them to get them to back off."

"Are they still bullying at Drake? I would think they'd outgrow that."

"Oh, yes. But now that I am a senior, it's better for everyone. Please don't tell anyone, but Mr. Whelan has been teaching defensive moves to the younger girls I send to him. There are a lot of men in the school who would get him in trouble for that, including the principal."

"This is disturbing, but you seem to have been handling it," said her father. "I won't bring it up until after you come home, but I will want know more."

"Yes, sir."

The door opened to admit Nurse Meadows.

"Happy Thanksgiving, everyone."

"Thank you, Nurse," said Martin. "Same to you."

"Sorry you have duty, Dawn," said Louise.

"But I'm glad you're here," said Katherine. "Mom, I'm stuffed. You think we could share some of that with the staff here?"

"Of course, dear. That's a wonderful idea." She stood and took the basket out to the nurses' station.

Boston University

"KATHERINE MARIAN MILLBANK!" Katherine's heart stopped. She paused and turned at the top of the stairs. "You get down here—now!"

She could count on the fingers of one hand how many times her mother had used her middle name–with fingers left over. Once when she was seven years old in second grade; the last time during her freshman year in high school. Both were during arguments that she had lost, stomping away from her mother in a fit.

Gone in a flash was the pleasant expectation of changing into her bicycle kit and riding to Cascade Canyon to shred trails on her mountain bike. After being off her bike all winter recovering from her injuries in the Lagunitas Challenge, her daily workouts meant the world to her.

She dropped her book bag at the landing and walked carefully downstairs.

Her mother stood in the hallway, opening the mail. Never a timid person, Louise Millbank held herself erect, with powerful shoulders, high cheekbones, and a pair of eyes that could terrify a soldier twice her weight. She had done just that as an Army nurse stationed in Korea, breaking up a fight outside the base enlisted club. The soldier who started it found himself on his back with her boot on his groin and an umbrella pressing into his ribs. She had released him to the MPs, then tended the wounds of the others.

Katherine stood slightly taller than her mother, but right now, she felt tiny. On a visceral level, she expected to be turned into a frog or some other reptile. The fact that her head knew that Louise Millbank could not *really* work magic provided no comfort to her soul.

Her mother held out a business-looking letter, holding the envelope face down. Katherine reached for the letter, and thought, *There's something wrong with Mom's scowl.*

The letterhead was from Boston University.

Dear Ms. Millbank…

"BU has accepted me! Omigod, a full scholarship." She squeaked and hugged her smiling mother in a vise-like grip. Together, they jumped up and down and spun in a circle.

"All those AP courses didn't hurt, eh?" Her mother stood back, holding her hands. "Congratulations, dear."

"Should we call Dad?" They both looked at the grandfather clock in the hall.

"Unless there's an emergency, he'll be on his way home soon. Were you going out this afternoon?"

"I was, but …" Her mother gave her the envelope.

"Go ride. I promise not to breathe a word to your father until you get back."

An hour later, Katherine stopped in the yard to rinse her bike with the garden hose. She parked the bike in the garage, removed her shoes, and went into the house. Her parents were talking in the living room. She was still high on endorphins from the downhill and the ride back. She forced herself to stop in the hall and focus.

"Be right down," she said as she ran up the stairs. After stretching and taking a shower, she donned jeans and a tee shirt. She went to the kitchen to mix a tumbler of protein drink. Hoping that the pounding of her heart did not show, she joined her parents in the living room. They each had a glass of white wine.

"Your mother has feathers in her mouth," said the cardiac surgeon. "She won't tell me what color canary she has swallowed, but she is bursting from it. Do you need to tell me something?"

Katherine took the letter from her back pocket and handed it to her father. She wiggled her toes inside her sneakers and wrung her hands behind her back as he read.

He stood, put down his wine and spread his arms. Katherine flew into his embrace. Louise joined them in a three-way hug.

The rest of the school year quickly became a hazy memory for Katherine: final essays, two more downhill races, graduation in the school auditorium, and packing for her new life. The family debated for two weeks how to deliver her to the university. In the end, they decided to ship her things to Massachusetts and fly across the country. Not driving would leave time for Louise and Martin to visit with Louise's mother before returning to San Anselmo. Katherine would stay with her grandmother until it was time to move into her dorm room.

Katherine had been born in Essex County, but she remembered only snippets of her life before the family moved to California in time for her sixth birthday. The emotional memory of vacations near Cape Ann melted into the most wonderful dreams until the day she accompanied her parents to San Francisco International Airport for the transcontinental flight. She picked out the peninsula below as the big jet circled before landing at Boston Logan Airport. Her grandmother met them at baggage claim. Soon she was moving into her mother's old room, while her parents unpacked in the guest room.

***

Katherine paused on the sidewalk on Bay State Road. The dormitory had obviously been a hotel. She could read the name "Sheraton" engraved in the concrete over the entrance. It was Shelton Hall now, because the man who bought the old Sheraton Hotel could not afford to replace all the letters of the big sign on the roof.

After a quick hug, her grandmother had driven away. Not for the first time, Katherine was grateful that she had only a suitcase. She pulled it into the building and climbed to the fourth floor. She had read about Eugene O'Neill's ghost haunting her floor, but she wasn't ready for the lights to be dimmer when she stepped through the fire door to the landing.

She pushed open the door to her room and almost knocked over a woman just inside.

"I'm sorry!"

The girl closed the door to the walk-in closet and stepped aside.

"We're gonna need to watch out for this closet door." She put out her hand. "Laura Silva." She smiled. The shape of her black eyes reminded Katherine of her own mother and grandmother. Shining black hair tied back tightly in a long braid. Not as tall as Katherine, but not short, either. Katherine shook her hand.

"Katherine Millbank. I promise I'll be careful from now on."

"I just got here, so the door problem is a surprise to me, too."

Katherine looked around. A bunk bed to the left, two small desks on the far wall, window between the desks and the beds.

"Did you pick a bunk? I've only ever had a bunk bed in summer camp."

"Not yet, but I would just as soon have the upper bunk. My brother was a noisy sleeper and got up a lot at night."

"Okay with me. We can switch later if you want."

"The resident assistant left a form on a clipboard for us to work out some details." She passed the clipboard on her desk to Katherine.

"Looks like a good start. Have you put away your things yet?"

"No. Let's do that, then do the list."

The list went some way as an ice breaker. Neither girl smoked. They both liked background music when studying (anything instrumental). They both had eye shades, not knowing what their routine would be like. Both heterosexual. No special boyfriend–yet. No opinion about having boys in the room.

"That will depend on the boys," said Katherine. "If they're as clueless or as annoying as the ones in high school, I won't be bringing anyone home."

Laura chuckled. "Me, neither."

***

Shelton Hall, 15 September

Dear Mom and Dad –

Greetings from the Boston Terrier's doghouse. My roommate, Laura Silva, is totally cool. She's from Gloucester, so I will probably get back to Essex County more often than I expected. The trolleys and buses make it easy to get around, but I miss my bike (hint, hint).

Our floor is called the Writers' Floor because of the famous authors who lived here as students, but it is also a specialty floor for English and Language majors—basically those of us who write. As you know, Shelton is a female dorm, but it's not like a convent or anything. The top floor has a big area for hanging out, and guys from other dorms come over. Before you think about it, I haven't been here long enough to meet anyone interesting yet. Our classmates seem as clueless as they were in high school. Eventually, I may meet upperclassmen and graduate students, especially at the Canterbury House. I've been once, and they seem like a fun bunch.

So far, all my classes are core liberal arts subjects: Physics 101, Calculus 201, English 201 and 301 (American Lit and Creative Writing), and French 202. I want to improve my French, because it's so easy to get to Québec from here (just dreaming; I won't run away yet!). With the credit they gave me for AP English, French and History, I could declare a major as early as next semester and start taking those courses. The professors taught the first classes in all our subjects, but normally we have teaching assistants twice a week and a lecture by the prof once. It works out. All the faculty and TAs have office hours, so there is lots of help. I have not needed any yet. Laura and I work to stay on top of the assignments, because there are so many, but they are not hard.

Laura is a runner, and I join her every morning. I love it. We usually run along the Charles River, where we can see the crew teams from Harvard, BU, and MIT working out on the water. Now I understand why you both told me how much you miss Boston.

Also, there is a pool in the athletic center, which we can use anytime. It's a proper natatorium, with bleachers and Olympic lanes and everything. Rosie Beauchamp, who lives next door, is a varsity swimmer, and we have started joining her on weekends for what we call our mini triathlons. So far just the three of us, but it has given me an idea. In the spring, there are marathons and regular triathlons here. I will let you know if I find something to fill the gap I feel when I miss the trails on Mount Tamalpais.

Dad, I've been thinking about your advice to pay attention to my body and my athletic performance. I'm not sure what you mean, but I find that I have to hold back to avoid losing Laura and Rosie. It has me concerned, because I never noticed when I was shredding trails with the guys in Cascade Canyon. When would be a good time to talk about this?

Gotta go. It's Friday night, and I promised Rosie and Laura to go see <u>Thelma and Louise</u>. Looking forward to it.

I'll write or call again. For what it's worth, you know I like to put pen to paper; this is a break from writing term papers and reports.

Your loving daughter,
Katherine.

***

"Hello?"

"Hi, Dad. Surprise! Laura and I got a phone."

"Katherine! That's wonderful." Martin motioned for Louise to pick up the cordless extension from the kitchen. "We were just starting dinner. Your mother is bringing the other phone to the table."

"Sorry to interrupt, but I was afraid to call too early or catch you out for the evening. Besides, you wrote that you didn't have regular commitments on Monday nights."

"Dear, this is a transcontinental long-distance call," said her mother.

"Nope. Remember those cellular bag phones the race officials used to coordinate the starts?"

"Yes?"

"Well, we went into the AT&T store on Commonwealth Avenue the other day and got a bag phone for just thirty dollars a month. Twenty-five is the monthly charge and five for the phone, so no up-front costs. We can call anywhere in the country for as long as we like.

"Here. Take down the number. 617-434-0540. It has voice mail, which picks up when we turn it off or are on the phone. That allows us to lock it up when we're in class, but not miss a call. Only Rosie and Laura are sharing it with me."

"When is a good time to call you?"

"I put my schedule with the letter I sent today. If I'm working on something and shouldn't talk, I'll let you know, because we know the phone could be a time-suck if we're not careful with it."

"Very smart, Katherine," said Martin, while Louise took a sip of her wine. "So, what did you want to talk about this time?"

"What you said about athletic performance. What did you mean?"

"Just that if you keep riding, running, and swimming as fast as you do, someone may notice and want to run tests on you. At the higher levels, there will be mandatory tests. Lots of blood samples. That sort of thing."

"So? I'm not afraid of needles, and they won't pull a full pint like the Red Cross, will they?"

"No, not at all. But when they can't find drugs or blood-doping indicators, the testers will be puzzled, and I wouldn't want you to become a celebrity in the medical research community – unless you want to, of course." There was silence on the line. "Katherine, are you there?"

"Yes, Dad. I was thinking. On the bulletin board in the cafeteria, I noticed how many graduate students and faculty advertise for volunteers for their studies. Everything from stress testing and videos of subjects running to balance testing. Almost all of them want bloodwork. Is that what you mean?"

"Well, yes and no. If the research study has a large sample, say, a hundred or more people, they would probably throw out your numbers as an outlier, because they're not looking to explain a specific race result. But the doctors at a sanctioned race would want to keep testing until they could explain why you can run, ride or swim so fast."

"What's an outlier?"

"It's a term from statistics. If you go for a PhD, you'll learn more than you want to know about it. Basically, it's a data point so far from the others that including it would skew the results. Outliers happen in statistical studies like the ones you described, so no big deal."

"I think I understand. Should I avoid those studies?"

"Follow your intuition. If there is one that interests you, you could at least make it clear that any release forms you sign are only for the specific research, not for additional testing. How does that sound?"

"I feel better, Dad."

"If you do this, Katherine, please have them give you the results. I expect your numbers to be unusual, but we'll add them to the rest of your medical file here."

"What are you thinking?"

"Nothing in particular. Data first, then hypothesis."

"Yeah, I've heard that before." Katherine smiled. "What I get for having you two as parents."

After agreeing that Katherine would call about the same time on Mondays, they ended the call.

***

The next morning, the three friends were running along the Charles River. It was a rare, sunny day, the air bracing cold, the winds calm, and no ice patches for a change. Katherine was matching their pace. She heard male voices chatting as they got louder.

"On your right!"

Katherine dropped behind Rosie to form a single file so the men could pass. It was a trio of boys, about the same age as the three girls. After the first two passed them, Katherine felt a hand squeeze her right buttock. The boy slapped Rosie and Laura on the butt as he ran to catch up his fellows.

"You sonofabitch!" Katherine shouted. A red haze came over her as her vision tunneled. She sprinted to the trio of men, grabbed the wise guy's arm and swung on it, wrenching it up and back. She heard him scream as he fell to the side of the path, then she was off. The shouting faded behind her.

Katherine did not slow until she reached the exit to the Essex Street bridge. Taking the stairs two at a time, she turned left and ran back to Shelton House on the sidewalk.

Laura and Rosie were just coming into the common area of their suite when Katherine came out of the shower room.

"Jeez, Katherine! What the hell came over you?"

"I don't know about you, but I don't put up with uninvited passes and other forms of sexual assault."

"That wasn't assault, but what you did—"

"Yes, it was. Last week, I smacked his arm when he tried to grab us and told him to keep his hands to himself. He probably thought it was funny."

"Oh. I didn't know."

"He was alone then. Probably thought he would impress his buddies today."

"He'll be okay," said Rosie. "His buddies chased you halfway to the bridge, then came back. By then, he could stand. He was working out his arm as they walked back."

Laura pushed into the room and held the door for Katherine.

"I didn't know you could run like that. Those guys nearly died trying to catch you." She began undressing to go to the shower. "Have you been holding back for us?"

"Well, yeah. But it's not like we're racing or anything, just running for the fun of it."

"But you're not getting as much of a workout as Rosie and I. We gotta find you a serious team."

***

The next night, Katherine called home. After telling her parents that she and Laura decided not to rush any sororities, she stopped.

"Katherine, are you there?"

"Yes, Dad. I've got some news, and I don't know if it's bad or not. The campus police came to see me this morning."

She told them about the boy who made a pass at the three girls, and what she had done to him.

"Katherine, your fuse is too short."

"Dad, I warned him last week, so he should have known better."

After a silence, he asked, "What did the police have to say?"

"When I explained that it was a repeat assault, they went away, promising to let me know the results of their investigation. They winced at the word 'assault,' because I know they were prepared to use it on me. But at orientation, we had a whole section on sexual assault, and this was clearly what they were talking about."

Her father made a noise. "You may not hear back."

"Are you alright, dear?"

"Yes, Mom. But sometimes the catcalls on the streets and the crude jokes in the cafeteria bug me. I'll finish my degree on an extension program in prison at this rate."

"I know how you feel. Do want some tips on handling it without getting arrested?" To her surprise, Katherine could hear her mother smiling.

"Mom? You?"

"I was an over-energetic girl once, you know. I never did learn my place."

"Right. So, what should I do?"

"You're going to spend Thanksgiving with your Gramma. Ask her for some advice. She has dealt with more than you will ever know."

"She has? My grandmother?"

"None other. You may get the same advice I got. And maybe she'll show you some tricks and moves she taught me. Give her my love."

Her father said, "That's better than anything I could think of, Katherine. Anything else for us?"

"I'm really glad to be so close to Gramma and my great aunts and uncles here, but I miss you both terribly."

"I wish we were there. We spent the best years of our lives in Boston."

"Martin, we need to go."

"Right. Katherine, how do you feel now?"

"Not scared or worried anymore. Thanks. I love you."

"Love you too."

Nigå

KATHERINE BOARDED THE NOON TRAIN to Rowley, to spend the long Thanksgiving weekend with her grandmother. She was intrigued and excited to spend some time alone with the impressive woman, especially since her mother had hinted that Marian Massey might have tips to help Katherine deal with unpleasant men—without running afoul of the authorities. That comment only intensified Katherine's curiosity…

Last summer, just before her freshman year, her parents had taken her to Essex County, where her mother, Louise, had grown up. Katherine moved into what had been her mother's childhood room in a two-story house in the Great Marsh North Wildlife Management Area. Surrounded by untamed woods, she heard only birds and animals at night, although if the wind blew from the west, sometimes they could faintly hear the commuter train passing through Rowley.

The two weeks that Louise and Martin had stayed in the house, the conversations had mostly revolved around Katherine and her future at Boston University. Martin answered countless questions from Marian about his work at the San Anselmo Medical Center. Louise endured detailed quizzing on her research on the languages of the Salish in the Pacific Northwest.

However, sometimes there would be long silences, or Katherine would walk in on a conversation, and the talk would cease, especially if her mother had been the one speaking. Marian or Martin would start up a conversation, but Katherine knew that they had changed the subject.

On the afternoon before her parents flew home to California, Katherine had seen her mother and grandmother walking toward the river. It looked like an argument, or at least a very emotional conversation, but she could not hear what they were saying. She watched the two women gesturing wildly, stopping to shout at each other.

When Marian slapped her daughter, Katherine gasped and watched in horror as the two women faced off in motionless silence. She held her breath, fully expecting Louise to strike back or worse.

She remembered seeing her mother break up a street fight one night in downtown San Anselmo. Both men were unconscious when the ambulance arrived.

The two women stood as straight as the trees around them, their braided hair falling down their backs, one auburn, the other silver. Katherine had never before appreciated just how very much alike they looked, in their movements, their gestures, and now in their power and pride.

When Katherine had almost run out of breath, she saw her mother drop to one knee and bow her head. *What the hell?* she thought. Marian reached out to put her hands on either side of her daughter's head. She raised up the younger woman, and they hugged each other.

Katherine's grandmother ran a hand down her mother's head and back while Louise shook as she sobbed…

As the train slowed, Katherine scanned the platform. She recognized the tall woman with large, dark eyes and a sharp, straight nose immediately. Marian Massey stood erect, her broad shoulders and smooth skin those of someone half her age. Last summer, Katherine had marvelled at the way her grandmother managed her house and garden by herself.

They hugged briefly but firmly. Marian stood back with her hands on Katherine's upper arms and ran her gaze up and down the young woman. She smiled approvingly at the hiking boots.

"Just the backpack?"

"As you suggested, Gramma."

"Good. Come." She turned and walked briskly along the right of way leading south from the station and over a bridge above the Egypt River. Katherine caught up and settled into an easy hiking pace. It helped that the two women had legs about the same length. They crossed the tracks after a half-mile. Salt marsh grasses and meandering creeks and streams spread out on either side of a faint path that divided the wetlands. Katherine's heart lifted as she watched the sun turn the brown grasses of the salt marsh into waving blankets of gold.

They did not speak, which Katherine did not mind, considering the blistering pace that her grandmother set for them. They walked toward a small wood. Canada geese flew in formation overhead, and waterbirds of different species went about finding supper, either diving into the water or ducking their heads suddenly. Occasionally, Katherine spotted the splash of a fish snatching insects flying near the surface. Her own stomach grumbled.

"I heard that," said the older woman, with a brief smile. "We'll have tea at the house—one of the few good things the English gave us."

For no reason she could discern, Katherine wondered who "us" was.

The darkness in the wood surprised Katherine. Almost immediately, she realized that the trail was better defined than she first realized. It seemed to be a game trail in the wildlife management area, but it was well-packed.

"Where is the road that we used last summer?" she asked. "I remember a long dirt driveway off Town Farm Road."

"Over yon." Her grandmother waved in the general direction of the sun. "This is more direct, and definitely faster." She led them through a patch of marsh and into the next wood. After a couple of right-angle turns, the path spilled onto a clearing in which stood the house that Katherine remembered.

The building was unchanged, but now Katherine took in more details. The parlor was bigger than she remembered, with more chairs than before. It resembled the meeting room of a conference center. Twenty or more people could sit around in the space.

"Same bedroom. Settle yourself while I put on the kettle. Come down when you're ready."

"Thank you, Gramma." She ran upstairs to unpack her backpack. She had cooled off quickly, so she decided not to take a shower until later.

Downstairs, she found her grandmother standing by the dining room table holding a teapot. Two places were set, with bone China cups, and plates with small sandwiches, pickles, cucumbers, and a plate of small scones.

"My goodness, a full English tea. You weren't kidding!"

"No, indeed. Alone, I generally have a mug of tea and a scone in the kitchen, but this is fun. Sit."

"I know you live alone, but isn't this place rather much to keep up by yourself?"

"Oh, I may live alone, but as you will see, I have plenty of help. Your cousins fall over each other to check on me and do things for me."

Katherine selected a sandwich and tasted the tea. "I can't imagine how nice that must be, having relatives close by."

"Moving to California was not easy for your mother, you know. Martin was also troubled, and almost turned down the job in San Anselmo." She smiled as she took a sandwich and put it on her plate. "From what I saw, you did not suffer much out there. Beautiful country."

"It is, and I love it, but now I wonder what we left behind. I know almost nothing about our relatives here. Mom goes silent on me when I ask. She always has."

"Well, you'll meet more of them than you can remember this weekend, and I promised your mother to give you some history lessons, if you'd like."

"I'd like that very much, Gramma."

"Good. Now, knowing you were coming, I told them to stay away until Thanksgiving dinner, so you can help me get ready. Shall we?" She rose and led Katherine to the kitchen.

The two women gathered, plucked, washed, sliced, diced, mashed, trimmed, marinated, baked, fried, grilled, and sautéed food into Wednesday night and all Thursday morning. All the traditional Thanksgiving items were on the menu. When Katherine noted that everything was

American (no rice, pasta or other European imports), her grandmother told her that the original so-called Thanksgiving had everything that they were making, and nothing else.

"It's all local, too."

"Even the meat?"

"Especially that. Shot the turkey and the deer myself after watching them fatten themselves among my corn."

"Is that legal? I mean, this is a wildlife management area, isn't it?"

"It is. And I am one of the managers, in a way. I'll explain after we feed the family. Saturday or Sunday, I think."

"Is that part of the history lessons?"

"Yes, it is." Marian paused her kneading. "That was your head I saw in the bedroom window when your mother and I came back from our long talk the last afternoon." She cocked an eyebrow.

Katherine blushed. "I'm sorry. I wasn't trying to spy. I just looked out the window, and there you both were."

"Don't worry about it. But I want you to form a first impression of your relatives before I tell you the story. Do you mind?"

"No. Thank you."

***

On Thursday morning, they pulled the dining room table into the big living room, inserted four table leaves, and set two dozen places. The colorful rugs, wall hangings and decorations on the walls turned the room into a banquet hall for a summit meeting.

About two p.m., the cousins, aunts, and uncles began arriving. Katherine met a blur of different people. Most did not offer their surnames, although there was at least one Massey, and one red-headed boy her own age was John Harwich, which she knew was her maternal grandfather's name. They called her grandmother Nigå, the same name her mother used. Since Marian was Louise's mother, Katherine guessed that nigå did not mean what she thought it did.

Some of them remembered the little tomboy who had played with their children. Those children included John and two women in their twenties. Katherine did not recognize anyone, but she noticed that she and John were the youngest people there.

"Bear. Is that a nickname for something?" She asked one heavyset man about her own height, with thick black hair. Black hair peeked out from the cuffs of his flannel shirt, also.

"Nope. I was baptized Bear Massey. Lots of bears in our family." He grinned and nudged one of the uncles. "Not many turtles, though." Katherine arched her eyebrows in a question. "He's Uncle Snapper, but only among us."

Katherine smiled and chuckled, hoping to hide the fact that she did not get it.

When everyone gathered around the table, Katherine found herself between John and Bear, who did not pause their friendly argument about the Bruins' chances against the Penguins until they noticed Nigå staring at them from the head of the table.

Marian Massey never looked so much like Katherine's idea of a matriarch as when the older woman stood tall, looked at the ceiling, then bowed her head, closed her eyes, and said, "Bless this food to our use and us to Thy service." She continued with ten or eleven lines in a language Katherine had never heard. Everyone said "Amen" when she stopped. Katherine recognized the familiar grace from the Book of Common Prayer, *but what followed it?*

The questions she had for her grandmother were piling up: the argument with her mother, the names of her cousins, the extra prayer, the hunting in the management area, the animal names of Bear and Snapper, the absence of a vehicle outside, her mother's comment, "I never did learn my place," and, if she wasn't reading too much into it, the deference of her relatives to their hostess.

It wasn't just good manners. They seemed to admire, love, and respect her, regardless of their age. Twice, she noticed a friendly disagreement end as both parties turned to Nigå and asked her what she thought. Katherine was amazed to see the old woman answer them as smoothly as if she had been part of the conversation, although she had been talking to Great Aunt Someone on her left at the time.

Katherine also noticed that there were only six males at the table. Two were John and his twin brother (thus, her cousins), two were brothers of one of the women, both in their forties, and only two were husbands, both in their fifties. Obviously, the latter two had grown up around these women, given the easy familiarity they showed with all of them.

Katherine detected no sexual overtones or emotional uneasiness anywhere. She had never seen a mixed group this big not have some kind of negative energy working somewhere. But then, these were all kin, something she was not used to seeing together in such numbers.

The sun was long down when the family rose as one and cleared the table. Marian took Katherine's arm and led her to a corner of the room. The two brothers quickly pulled out the leaves of the table, moved it back to the dining room, and made the leaves vanish into a storage closet in the wall.

"I'll help with the dishes," said Katherine.

"No. We cooked. Others will clean up. Here, sit."

Some women had pulled the chairs into position. Others brought out the coffeemaker and set it on the sideboard, with mugs and the usual cream and sugar. One of the older aunts brought out the teapot, another the cups and fixings.

While the happy sounds of the men ribbing one another mingled with the clatter of pans and dishes and the sound of the sprayer in the kitchen sink, Katherine and the women sat in the living room.

Katherine worried about what she might be expected to say or do, but no one spoke. Eighteen women, ranging in age from eighteen to more than seventy rested with smiles or straight faces, as if nothing were more important in this moment than to simply relax.

Katherine's tea hadn't cooled when the six men joined the others in the living room, pausing at the sideboard for coffee or tea. The two boys exchanged silent smiles as they stopped giggling about the last joke in the kitchen. The men sat with sighs or letting out a breath as they, too, settled into a relaxed mood after the meal.

It came to her then, in her mother's voice, "Sometimes, there is nothing more blessed than to sit calmly and do nothing."

Katherine stopped looking around and let the peace of the family envelop her. She stared at the mantle of the fireplace, letting it go out of focus as she cleared her mind.

Before she nodded off from too much turkey and relaxation, she heard her grandmother say, "Anyone?"

John spoke up. "Tell us a story, Nigå."

"Before or after?"

"Before, please." His eyes shone with excitement, and the others leaned in to listen.

Nigå took a deep breath, then stared out the window for a time. When she spoke, her voice carried time, space, smells, and sounds. Her listeners did not move.

In the time before the white man came, your many-times-grandmother guided her people from the top of the hill that overlooked Agawam from the sea. Back then, the Great Marsh had not flooded as much as it has today, so one could walk to Agawam almost in a straight line. Plum Island was not an island, but connected to the shore at its north end, and the Merrimack River flowed past it.

In the late winter one year, a messenger came from the sågamå of the Abenaki Confederacy, announcing a powwow after the harvest, before the snows would begin. The raids between the Penacook and the Abenaki had turned ugly, and the Eastern Abenaki were restless. Being so far south, we had not been very active with our cousins north of the Merrimack. For the sågamå to call a caucus meant that the confederacy could fall apart if consensus over the various claims could not be found. Our saunksqua was greatly respected by the sågamåk of the other tribes, having been re-elected many times since her first husband died when she had seen only twenty harvests. Her name up north was "the Peacemaker", but so far, she had only helped settle disputes between individuals and small groups. She told the messenger to tell the sågamå that she would attend with our sachem and a small band of hunters..."

Katherine listened spellbound, but her head was spinning. The "us" must be the Pawtucket, which she thought were related to the Wampanoag and Massachusett. Who were these cousins and aunts and uncles? What were these titles? *And what am I?*

... For many years after that, she continued to turn down requests from the sågamå to stand for election at the confederacy, so that he got the nickname Almisaosat. His people liked him, though, so he wore the name with pride.

"Do you know what an almisaosat is?" Nigå asked John.

"A chief on the way out."

"Lame duck," said his brother, causing laughter among the adults.

Nigå smiled and stood. "This has been a wonderful day for me. Thank you for coming, and please drive carefully." She walked to the front door. Everyone rose and followed her.

Katherine's cousins, aunts, and uncles stopped to hug her in the hall before hugging Marian on their way out.

Katherine went into the parlor to take the coffee and tea things back to the kitchen, but someone had already done that. They were in the drying rack by the sink.

"Well, how was your Thanksgiving?" Her grandmother stood at the kitchen door.

"I'm stunned. My mother did not explain this to me." She paused. "Am I an Indian?"

"If by that you mean the First Nations, the indigenous people, or as the other nations call us, the Dawn People, yes.

But there is much more to it than that. I'm glad young John chose a story from the Before times. Most of the After stories are not happy ones." She straightened a dish towel hanging on the oven door handle. "Let's take a long walk tomorrow. And maybe the rest of the weekend. I have more than history to tell you, and some questions to ask."

"Of course. Let's."

"Good night, then. Sleep tight, *Noses*."

"Good night, Nigå."

They hugged briefly, then walked upstairs silently. Twenty minutes later, the house lay still among the sounds of the nocturnal animals in the Marsh.

An Origin Story

FRIDAY OF THE THANKSGIVING WEEKEND burst into the window with a brilliant dawn that woke Katherine suddenly as the sun leapt from the ridge of Plum Island. She went to the window. Frozen dew shone among the trees. The grasses in the Great Marsh stood still, like a crowd waiting to worship the great ball rising over them. She watched the dew vanish as the light struck the trees and the reeds. This would be a memorable autumn day: clear, cold, crisp, but comfortable in the sunshine.

Her grandmother promised to explain her history to her today. Her heart sped up as she considered the emotions that came with that thought. Excitement–to discover that her family was here when the colonists arrived; surprise–she was still reeling from the discovery that she was Pawtucket, not English or some other European nation. Her initial anger that her mother had hid this from her had subsided into mere annoyance.

She heard the gurgle of the coffeemaker downstairs. She used the bathroom, then dressed quickly in long underwear, jeans, and a flannel shirt. In the kitchen, her grandmother was transferring flapjacks from an iron skillet to a plate. The table was set for two.

Her grandmother also wore flannel and jeans. Her silver hair fell in a long braid down her back. The older woman ran her gaze up and down and smiled approvingly.

"There's honey in that cupboard and milk in the refrigerator. Would you put them out, please?"

"Of course."

As they sat, Marian asked, "What do you want to know first?"

"I don't know where to start. Is what you have to tell me what you and Mom argued about when I saw you from the bedroom window last summer?"

"Yes, though I think she would agree that it was not an argument. It was a reconciliation that had been a long time coming."

"Mom told me that John Harwich was her father, but he died before she was born. Why isn't her maiden name Harwich?"

"John and I were duly married and deeply in love. He died when I was four months along, a month shy of our seventh anniversary. I was not rejecting John's name; our identity comes from our mothers."

"I gathered that we are Pawtucket, which I thought were extinct. Aren't the Pawtucket related to the Massachusett and the Wampanoag?"

"That's the Patuxet, a band that lived near where Plymouth is today. They did belong to the Wampanoag Confederacy. However, the Pawtucket descended from the Penacook, part of the Abenaki Confederacy, which you heard about in the story yesterday. Our language is a dialect of Western Abenaki. Most of the surviving Abenaki live in Canada, and the three states north of here." She rose and began clearing the table. "Let's take that walk."

The dishes done, they donned their hiking boots. With their walking sticks and empty backpacks, the two women set out through the woods, retracing their way to Rowley. Marian set a relaxed pace, so that they could talk.

"You will find only some of what I am telling you in printed sources, although I encourage you to read as much as you can about the history of the Pawtucket and the Abenaki tribes, especially before the Europeans arrived."

"That's the 'before times', I guess. 1620, the *Mayflower* and all that."

"Actually, the Dutch and the French got here first, and we were trading with them before the English arrived."

"I read that there was a smallpox epidemic, but now I realize that was a story about the Pilgrims and the Patuxet, who were south of here. What happened?"

"Our history goes back at least ten thousand years, when humans first walked in North America. By the time of European contact, there were three main cultural and linguistic groups here in the east: the Algonquin, called the Dawn People by the others, the Iroquois along the south of the Great Lakes, and the Sioux on the Great Plains. By the time the Pawtucket settled the coast, the Ice Age was retreating. The large mammals died out. Adapting to the changing climate is how we became farmers and fishermen instead of big game hunters.

"Until the American Civil War, the tribes were recognized as sovereign peoples, dealing with the Europeans then the Americans through treaties. That relationship held even though ninety percent of the Native population perished to leptospirosis, smallpox, and cholera. The epidemic of 1633 was particularly brutal, and that is usually the date given for the disappearance of our people."

"Not everyone died, though." Katherine turned her head to admire the proud woman walking at her side.

"No. You need to know how we were organized to understand why we went underground, so to speak. Each Pawtucket traces his or her origin to a single ancestor. That totem is how we identify ourselves. Ours is the bear."

"As in Bear Massey? I take it that Uncle Snapper is one of the turtles."

Her grandmother grinned and nodded. "In the seventeenth century, Europeans were pushing hard to convert us to Christianity. As we died off, the survivors gathered in towns where the so-called Praying Indians had settled. Europeans took over our lands.

"The English thought that our sågamåk and sachems were leaders like their rulers, but we rule ourselves by consensus. Sågamå means "the one who prevails" not king or ruler. The role of the sågamå is to mediate, to facilitate consensus, and to resolve disputes.

"The Europeans assumed that we had a patriarchal society like theirs, so they overlooked or ignored the saunksquak among us. They also expected a sågamå to be responsible for the actions of the individuals in the tribe, which led to fatal misunderstandings. We were not a tribe in the European sense of tribes, clans, or other hierarchies. The sågamå had no authority over someone being abused by an Englishman, who chose to fight back.

"When the epidemics of the early seventeenth century tore through the land, your five- or six-times great grandmother was our saunksqua. We could see where history was taking us. By the summer of 1635, there were only a handful of survivors, all women, elites of the Bear clan. We slipped into the forest to the west and walked to the nearest praying town. The women swore to stay in touch, and to consult each other going forward.

"Most important, we chose our mates carefully, steering clear of men who embraced the attitudes of the Europeans. Before any of the women married, they would get the opinion of the others, to ensure that they all agreed that the man would make a worthy, equal partner. Three of the men had the surname Massey, though they weren't related. They were from the Massachusett people, nephews of the Massatoit in Rhode Island."

"Hence, all the Masseys."

"Yes. We knew that any so-called tribe that the colonial or American government would recognize would be a male-dominated hierarchy with no place for women. In effect, the Europeans drove us to form a secret sisterhood, but it is not a new organization. It's simply that the Pawtucket continue to operate as we did before the Contact. We raised our boys and girls to fit into their roles naturally. Some of the boys grew up to be sågamåk over the next three hundred years. My own father, for example. Because all the women in 1635 were Pawtucket, all those relatives you saw yesterday are Pawtucket today. We could never explain our matrilineal system to the Bureau of Indian Affairs under today's laws. It's not even matrilineal really. Our language does not have gender words, so males and females are the same."

"The Jews pass their identity through the mother."

"So do we. Paternity may always be challenged, but not birth."

"My cousins called you Nigå, which when I looked it up translates as 'grandmother'. Mom calls you that, but you're not her grandmother."

"We don't have a word for grandmother. Nigå means 'old one' and it is a title of respect. We call our parents and grandparents nigå, but also our aunts–any elder."

They had reached the commuter rail tracks. After crossing the river, they turned south and walked to a grocery store west of the tracks. Marian selected milk, flour, and other staples, which fit into their two backpacks.

"Let me get this, Gramma."

"No, Noses. You're the scholarship student without a job. I have my pensions and nothing to spend them on."

"Well, okay, but I'd like to treat you somehow when you come to Boston."

"Fine. I look forward to it."

"You called me 'noses' yesterday, too. What is that?"

"My grandchild."

They turned north and walked up Main Street. Katherine thought it strange that so many people smiled and greeted them. *I never see this kind of open friendliness in Boston,* she thought. Every third or fourth woman they passed–and all the men–also nodded respectfully.

"Are we so strange, Gramma? Those children looked at you with their jaws hanging."

Marian laughed. "The Turners? They're cousins of yours. Their mother probably tells them terrifying stories of what the saunksqua will do to them with her stick if they misbehave."

"You're kidding!" Katherine pulled her own jaw back up.

"Think about it. How do you get a child that young to internalize correct behavior? We can't use physical punishment, because they aren't old enough to understand action and consequence. But tell them a good story about something powerful that a nigå did, and they will instinctively mind that elder for the rest of their lives."

"No one spanks them?"

"I didn't say that. When they are older and make bad choices knowing the consequences, then punishment can work. Thanks to the early behavior, though, belts and switches are applied rarely."

"Do you always carry that walking stick?"

"Most of the time. Apart from the convenience, it has become part of my identity, don't you think?"

"To those little ones, certainly."

"And their mothers and fathers, too. I've been saunksqua for more than thirty years."

Marian pointed to a café at the edge of the downtown Rowley. They found a table in a corner away from the door.

"How secret is the tribe today?"

"We don't think of ourselves as a tribe, we are *Ninnuok,* which translates as 'the People here.' We're not secret, just unofficial. We try not to discuss the People with outsiders. As far as they are concerned, we are part of the general population. Our youngsters grow up knowing that this discretion protects the band and their family."

"How do you keep a boy from blabbing to his classmates in school?"

"Before they ever go to school, they internalize the discretion. The importance of their initiation when they reach puberty looms big in their lives, and what child does not love knowing a secret? Almost everyone around here has some Native DNA, so it's not a big deal to be an Indian." She put air quotes on the word. "It's the fact that the Pawtucket still exist as a group that we don't volunteer. There is no point in seeking recognition, when the American paradigm that replaced the European one is worse."

"I think I get it. I just don't understand why Mom never told me."

Marian reached across and took Katherine's hand.

"Your mother was your age when she left. Can you picture that?"

"To join the Army."

Marian let go and sat back. "Then went to college on the GI Bill—in California. If she had not done graduate school in Cambridge, she might never have come home again. As it is, when she and Martin fell in love, it was a blessing. He is the kind of man we encourage our girls to find."

"But he's not wimpy or anything like that."

"No. He is a true, equal, and supportive partner. Wouldn't you agree?"

Katherine thought a while, and her gaze went out the window. "Yes." She looked back at her grandmother. "Now I see that he's the reason most men tick me off. I know what they could be like, but they're not." She sipped her coffee. "So, why not tell me about us?"

"When Louise left, she *really* left. Picture the personalities involved."

"Mom said that she was an over-energetic girl who never knew her place."

"So was I. Imagine it." She held Katherine's gaze and let the picture rise between them.

As they looked at each other, a soft giggle grew to hearty laughter. When the people at the other tables turned around, they struggled to control themselves.

"It's funny now, but until last summer, neither of us could have laughed. It was Martin who brought her back. Look how long it took him."

"Is she a one of the Ninnuok or not?"

"She is Pawtucket, she can't change that. But she did leave it all behind. Whether she remembers the language, or would want to embrace us again, I don't know." Marian rose. They took their mugs and plates to the bussing station. "Now that we are comfortable with each other again, we can look forward to whatever will happen while you are in college. Your parents could not come see you without coming here, could they?"

"No." She snorted. "When they come east to see me, I'm likely to be here, not at school."

They shouldered their packs, and continued north on Main Street, taking a right onto Railroad Avenue. As they passed the train station and followed the railroad right-of-way and game trails, Marian identified the saunksqua in each generation, the men they married, who moved away and who stayed, which children grew up locally, and which moved on. Some of the boys became sågamåk, but over three hundred years, there were less than a dozen of them. The women stayed in touch, so that Marian had a network of contacts in forty-five states.

The shadows were long by the time they emerged from the woods near the house.

"I must be related to almost everyone between Newbury and Gloucester," said Katherine.

"You probably are. Not many of them know it, though."

They made a small supper using leftovers and turned in early. Katherine noticed that her grandmother took a book to her room, so the older woman was probably not as tired from all the walking as the teenager.

Katherine lay in bed, savoring the silence. *No, not the silence,* she thought, *the absence of noise.* No engines, no cars, no trains, no buzzing high-voltage lines or neon signs. Instead, she listened to the call of a wild creature in the night, the plop of some amphibian jumping in the water, or the hoot of an owl.

*****

The sun woke her again. She stretched and breathed deeply. In the late fall, the air over the Marsh carried no unpleasant odors, and this far from the settled areas, there were no smells of so-called civilization. Katherine thought of the cold air on Mount Tamalpais and the woods of the Samuel Taylor State Park. She said a silent prayer of thanksgiving for the unspoiled, clean places that she had known growing up.

After breakfast, they sat in the kitchen. Katherine asked, "Do have any chores I could help with?"

"Not really. I had a stream of young men and women here all month helping me get ready for the winter. Bear Massey even chopped all that wood you see behind the house."

"If you say so. I just want to be helpful."

"Tell you what. We do have to take the trash and recycling to the Ipswich Transfer Station. I won't have to make two trips if you take half."

"Let's. Where is it?"

"Grab your hiking boots and that pair of work gloves on the counter. Come."

Behind the house next to the woodshed, two four-sided carts sat next to the ubiquitous green and blue bins from the county. The carts were big, with long handles that looked like the traces of a wagon.

"Where's the pony to pull those?"

Marian laughed. "Put on the gloves and neigh." She rolled one of the bins to a cart, dropped the back of the cart and pushed the bin into the cart. She closed the back gate of the cart, securing the bin in the cart. "Now the other one."

Katherine pulled the other bin to its cart and imitated her grandmother.

"Do you walk to the transfer station?"

"Of course. It's less than a mile to the end of Town Farm Road, then about five hundred yards to the station itself."

Katherine held her amazement to herself as she followed her grandmother into the woods south of the house. They were on the narrow, dirt road that Katherine remembered from last summer, barely wide enough for a car. In just a hundred yards, they came out of the woods.

The dirt track led them between a small, wooded hill and the inlets from Shad Creek. It was level, and the fat tires on the carts made pulling them easy. In less than a half hour, they were dipping the bins into the appropriate dumpsters at the transfer station. Marian introduced Katherine to the station operator, a solid man in his fifties, who introduced them to his grandson. Jeb and Petey Massey: Marian nodded when Katherine glanced at her.

"Petey here has applied to the County for three different maintenance jobs," said Jeb. "I've been showing him this operation."

"Good for you, Petey," said Marian. "Do you need a recommendation or a reference?"

"I've got plenty now, Nigå, but one from you would be awesome. Thank you."

"Can I send it to you, or do I need to give it to HR in town?"

"If you call me, I can come get it, ma'am."

"I'll call you next week, then. Good luck."

A half-hour later, they stowed the carts and bins by the woodshed, and walked into the house. Katherine brought in some wood to fill the canvas carrier by the fireplace and the wood box by the stove. They changed out of their work boots on the porch. Katherine stocked the firewood by the stove and fireplace, while Marian put the kettle on.

"How long has this house been here?" Katherine asked as they relaxed in a pair of stuffed chairs in the living room.

"This is the third or fourth house, actually. Our main village was on Castle Hill as you heard the other day. Most of the fishing folk lived down here in the Great Marsh. After the 1635 epidemic, there was only one wigwam here, occupied by those who came back from the praying towns. We kept a presence here, because the fishing was good, and we could dry and salt the fish before bringing it inland to trade. The English were not interested in the deep marsh, so it was a good place for staying out of sight."

"You mean my many-times-grandmothers and their kin?"

"Yes. You and Louise descend directly from the handful of Pawtucket who came back after the epidemics and made a living fishing.

"To answer your question, the first house went up just after the American Revolution, about 1785. It burned down because it wasn't made well. We lived in wigwams until about 1812. By then, enough of us had gone to school and learned European and American building methods to build a one-story, two-room house. It was invisible in the wood, and it was a year-round shelter. My grandmother tore it down to build this house, which would have been about 1899."

"Not your grandfather?"

Marian smiled. "He died before that. Mother was three when they started, and it took them twelve years to finish it. By then, my mother knew everything about building and maintaining a house. She made me learn everything, from pouring concrete and building a chimney to making lumber from trees. I've been lucky that so many cool machines have been invented in my lifetime, and that you can rent the bigger ones when you need them."

Katherine looked around the room in awe. "That mantle? The chimney? These beautiful oak floors?"

"And most of the furniture. Nigå and my mother made them all. I built the woodshed and the carts. Would you like to go fishing this afternoon?"

"You have a boat, too?"

"Of course. We're fisherfolk, after all. And, yes, I built it."

Marian rose and led Katherine into the kitchen to fix lunch.

***

As they returned to the pier, a ranger was standing in the clearing. He seemed only a little older than Katherine. He stood with his arms crossed as they slid along the pier and tied up.

"A new one," Marian mumbled. "Here. Hold the fish." She handed Katherine the bag with the four large fish in it.

The ranger came to the pier.

"Good afternoon, ladies. You must have seen the sign." He pointed to the white sign by the pier. "No fishing or hunting."

"Of course," said Marian. "And you must be new here. I'm Marian Massey, and you are?"

"Er – Ranger Bowditch." He seemed stymied by Marian's confident courtesy.

"Pleased to meet you. I take it that Superintendent Arthur and Ranger Medford have not briefed you."

"About what?"

Marian pointed to the white sign below the No Fishing sign. "Residents Only. No trespassing."

"We live here, Mr. Bowditch. Do come in and have some tea."

"But—"

"Relax, young man. My granddaughter won't knock you out with a fish, and I'll be happy to explain us to you. Come." She marched up to the house, leaving the surprised ranger to follow in her wake. Katherine bit the inside of her mouth to keep from grinning or laughing.

Thomas Bowditch had just reported, and as the newest ranger, he had pulled the long duty weekend. He was stunned to learn that Marian's family had lived in the marsh for centuries. They could hunt and fish without a license and enjoyed unrestricted access to the wildlife management area.

"Have Mr. Medford show you the maps next week," said Marian, as she poured his tea. "You'll see how we conveyed most of the Marsh to the State to keep it from development. A win-win for both sides."

"Do you mean you can drive in the management area?"

"We could, but we don't. You'll have noticed the lack of any motor vehicle outside, and my boat is powered by oars. By the same token, I hope you left your ATV at the end of Town Farm Road. Even the rangers are not to bring those things into the Marsh. They disturb the wildlife."

Bowditch blushed. "I didn't know."

Marian made a noise. "I won't mention it to Arthur or Medford next week, but please don't bring the ATV back in the future."

He left after finishing his tea and one scone. Katherine and Marian giggled as they walked to the kitchen to clean the fish and put three of them in the freezer.

***

Sunday morning at first light, Katherine came down to find herself alone in the house. The coffee had been made and there was fresh bread for toast. She poured herself a cup, then walked around the ground floor. In the hall, she slipped into her coat and stepped out on the porch.

Her grandmother sat on her heels at the edge of the clearing near the pier, facing away from the house. She wore only a long buckskin tunic, and her feet were bare. As the upper limb of the sun appeared over Plum Island, she rose to a kneeling position. Katherine could hear a song (*a hymn?*) in the language she had heard at Thanksgiving dinner. Marian sang one verse on her knees, then stood in a single fluid motion and sang another verse with her arms extended. The saunksqua then dropped her arms and turned around. She smiled at Katherine as she walked back to the house.

"Did you want to go to church? Ascension is just three miles away at the other end of Town Farm Road."

"I think I have just been. Would you teach me that song and explain it?"

"Let me get some hot coffee, if you left some."

Over toast and honey, Marian taught her granddaughter several prayers and songs of thanksgiving in the Pawtucket language. The sense of connection to the natural world gave the prayers more depth than Katherine had ever felt in church. She hungered to know more.

She brought up the encounters she had with touchy boys at school. "Mom said to ask you about how to handle them and keep from getting arrested."

"Ah, yes. Your mother had the same problem in high school. As did I before her." She finished her coffee. "Come." They went into the living room.

For the next hour, Marian drilled Katherine in simple moves that would immobilize or put off an assailant. Some were guaranteed to get attention, like shoulder dislocations, crushed testicles, and bloody noses. Others involved backing up fingers hard into the assailant's body, along with whispered threats in their ear. Trips, both obvious and sneaky. Elbows in places that ranged from painful to deadly.

"You can be as discrete as you want. Saving the male some face might make him behave in the future, instead of reporting you, or coming back with some thuggish friends. Just you and he need ever know who's boss."

Katherine rubbed the sore spot on her ribs. "What if I face a deadly threat? Like a mugging or the thugs do come back?"

"First, remember that most muggers do not intend to kill their marks, unless they're drug-crazed, so learn to tell the difference. Then, carry some wampum."

"Huh?"

Marian pulled a three-inch shell from her pocket. "I don't carry this all the time, but if you must go into a dangerous situation, you should know how to use it. Here." She handed the shell to Katherine.

The shell had been carefully filed and sanded so that the outside edge was smooth and razor-sharp.

"An oyster?"

"A big one or a scallop. You hold it like this." Marian showed her how to grasp the shell and then how to move it. "From behind, you could slice the jugular of a sentry before he ever knew you were there. But it's an effective knife from any direction."

"Omigod, Gramma. How or why did you learn this?"

"Now that you know our history, it should be obvious. Various authorities have forbidden us to carry weapons since colonial times. Who would suspect an Indian—especially a woman—with an oyster shell in her pocket? Even today's metal detectors would miss that." She took out a crescent-shaped piece of leather. "This is a sheath to keep it from cutting through your clothes."

"I wondered about that."

***

That afternoon, Katherine and Marian walked to the station at Rowley. The nigå planned to spend the night with a nephew who lived near town.

On the platform, Katherine hugged her grandmother.

"Nigå, I can't wait to come back in January before the second semester starts."

"I look forward to it. I have much to teach you, Noses."

"You think I can learn Pawtucket by the time I graduate?"

"Before that—and many other things, too. Be well and give my love to Louise and Martin."

Snowflakes drifted down as Katherine boarded the train.

In her dorm room at Shelton House, the young Pawtucket went to bed with centuries of intrepid women populating her dreams and her imagination. She had never felt so empowered in her life.

The Budding Scholar

KATHERINE SHOOK THE WATER off her jacket and rolled it up so it would not drip on the floor. She pushed through the door and climbed to the middle rows of the lecture hall. The back rows were taken.

The professor was standing in front of the long desk below the blackboard. Reginald Ardmore seemed younger than most of the professors she had met so far, his brown hair cut stylishly, his posture erect, a turtleneck under his sport coat. As far back as she was sitting, Katherine could not be sure of his eye color, but his face moved with expression. *As a tenured professor, he should be as old as my parents,* she thought, *or is he?*

Ardmore stood still and looked around, passing his gaze on each student individually. The hall fell quiet.

"The syllabus calls for us to cover the defining elements of Southern writers, but I want to canvass you about something else first." He walked around the desk and stopped at the blackboard. "Please raise your hand if you have read a book by a woman in the last, say, six years. Young Adult literature and up, so not children's authors. Let's say Keene, Collins, and Roth at the younger end." He paused. "If you don't remember the author's surname, she

80

did not make enough of an impression on you, so don't raise your hand.

"This is a literature class. Do I need to specify books? Movies and TV don't count." He smiled as chuckles floated around the room.

Katherine raised her hand. She guessed that half the hands went up. She thought the percentage should have been higher. This was a class for English majors, and there were more women than men in the room.

Professor Ardmore pointed to the raised hands one by one. As each student gave one or more names, he wrote them on the board. When he disallowed "Nancy Drew" as not being the author's name, a few hands went down quietly. When he finished, he dropped the chalk onto the ledge where it belonged and motioned to a boy in the front row to write down the list.

"This exercise has several purposes, some for me and some for you. Any thoughts?"

A redhead in the second row raised her hand. "Pay attention to what's around the story, like the author's name and maybe the other books she wrote." She had been the one who offered "Nancy Drew." Others had mentioned Carolyn Keene, so Katherine understood why Professor Ardmore did not make anything of the mistake.

He took another four comments. Katherine wondered if he were researching female authors for some reason. They were the focus of her own late-night forays, so she wanted to talk to him in private.

***

Katherine knocked on the wall next to the open door. Larry Steinmetz was bent over a notebook, writing furiously. He finished the line and slammed the pen down. The teaching assistants who shared the office were out.

"Ah, Miss Millbank, come in!" He pushed his unruly black curls out of the way and motioned to the chair. The smile included his very deep blue eyes. "I did not expect to see you here, considering your grades in this class. I love reading your work."

Katherine blushed. "Thank you, sir. I hope the critics are as receptive someday."

He chuckled at that. "They will be, I'm sure. You can call me Larry outside class."

"Actually, I want to see Professor Ardmore, but you're the section leader, so I thought I should bounce the idea off you first."

He stood. "Coffee? I just made it." He nodded to the Mr. Coffee machine on a file cabinet.

"Thanks. Black, please."

He brought two mugs back to the desk. "What can I help you with?"

Katherine blew on her coffee. "Have you noticed something missing in the curriculum? In particular, the list of authors we must read?"

Larry thought for a minute. "If I remember my Lit classes correctly, they were all dead white men."

"Exactly. Why no women? There's no shortage of them in the nineteenth or twentieth century."

"My mind is jumping ahead already. Ardmore would tell you that they must choose the very best authors. They can't include everyone."

"Not even Brontë, Austen, and Alcott?"

"I can hear them now: 'fluff, my dear, airheaded romance'." He mimicked a particularly pompous teacher they knew, which made Katherine chuckle.

"As far as I can tell from the class catalogs and syllabi back to 1951, the reading list for undergraduate English courses has not changed in forty years." She sipped her coffee. "Would I be amiss to suggest that the incumbents don't want to learn about women writers?"

Larry chuckled. "No. You might be spot on, except for some of our female faculty and the younger men. But they don't get to vote on such things."

"What if research in journals like *College English* proposed a curriculum?"

"I haven't seen anything like that."

"If I wrote it, do you think one of the journals would publish it?"

Larry almost spilled his coffee. He set down his mug and looked out the window.

"I never heard of an undergraduate publishing in a scholarly journal, but there is no law against it." He looked back at Katherine. "And if any undergraduate could write it, you could. The editor would be the only one to know who you are—assuming that the editor accepted the manuscript for peer review. He or she might wonder why your own school isn't implementing your curriculum."

"Do you think it would enough for me to say that BU is staffing the proposal? I would, of course, submit a formal proposal through the Department of English."

Larry laughed. "Then we could take bets on which happens first: article rejected, or proposal turned down." He turned serious. "Kidding aside. I think it's a great idea. This school has a history of trouble-making students bringing about change."

Katherine smiled. Larry made her feel comfortable, as if sharing a joke rather than a put-down.

"Should I see Professor Ardmore before I write the article and the proposal?"

Larry got up to fetch the carafe and refilled their mugs.

"My hunch is to write enough of the proposal to show him what it will look like. You need to submit it to him as course director anyway. Whether to share the article with him is a decision you can make while you are preparing the proposal. Do you need some help?"

"Not yet. I'll need a reviewer, and I may need sponsorship from a teacher for the proposal or the article. I'll let you know."

"I'd be happy to work on it with you. This could be fun." They finished their coffee talking about the respective mindsets needed to write short stories and novels. Then Katherine excused herself to return to Shelton Hall.

***

When Katherine came back from the Christmas break, she found an envelope from the English Department in her student mailbox. Laura was reading in her bunk.

"Has California slid into the ocean yet?"

"No, but not for lack of trying. It rained almost every day. Mud everywhere."

"Whatcha got there?" She looked at the envelope.

"I don't know." Katherine set down her suitcase, then sat at her desk. She opened the envelope with the letter opener she kept in a caddy on the desk.

"Professor Ardmore wants to see me."

"Does it say why? He was elected chair during the break, y'know."

"No, I didn't. What happened to Mangano?"

"Retired suddenly. Remember the stories about his falling asleep in meetings? He has CLL."

"Chronic lymphocytic leukemia?"

"Oh, is that what it means? According to Rosie, that's why he was tired all the time."

"I feel sorry for him. He took some flak for letting me declare a major in my freshman year."

"I'm sorry, too." She closed her book. "So, the new chair wants to see you on his first day in the job. Probably that proposal."

"Why wouldn't he say so in the letter? I left it off just before I flew home, so I don't imagine he's read it yet."

Katherine used their bag phone to call the department office. The chairman's secretary gave her an appointment for ten o'clock the next day, but also confirmed that she did not know what the meeting was about.

By the time Katherine walked to the English Department office after her first class, she had imagined herself into a near-panic. She paused in the hall to make herself breathe slowly. When her pulse returned to normal, she took a final breath and pushed open the door.

The secretary, a black-haired, blue-eyed Irish woman from North Boston, smiled broadly. Katherine liked Maria O'Hallaran, who had been her main point of contact when she was pushing the bureaucracy to let her declare a major in her first year.

"Hello, Miss Millbank. He's just finishing with another student." She motioned to a seat across from her desk. The door to the chairman's office opened. Katherine watched the football player, whose name she did not remember, walk to the hall with his jaw set and his eyes focused straight ahead. Professor Ardmore stood in his doorway, watching the man leave.

Katherine stood. The chairman smiled, and waved her in. Maria winked at her and grinned as she went by.

Katherine paused just inside. The walls still held Professor Mangano's diplomas and pictures, and the desk was covered with files and papers. The shelves held the same books that were there when Mangano interviewed her before Christmas. A pair of cardboard boxes occupied one corner, behind the door. A conference table to the right held file boxes and piles of papers, as well as what were clearly the new chairman's books.

"Please, have a seat." Ardmore indicated one of the two chairs in front of the desk, then took the other chair, allowing about four feet between their knees. This put one of the piles of folders close to him. "Please excuse the mess. I'm operating off the desktop and the table until we finish going through the files. Care for coffee or something else?"

"Coffee would be nice, sir." Katherine held her hands in her lap, not sure what to do with them. He smiled, and she noticed that his eyes were hazel, like hers. He reached for the phone and punched a button.

"Maria, sorry to disturb you, but I want to get started. Could we have some coffee? Black for me, of course." He raised his eyebrows at Katherine, who nodded. "Both black. Thanks." He replaced the handset. "I'm not used to having a secretary. I'll get my own coffeemaker as soon as I can."

He looked at her intently. She squeezed her hands together to keep from squirming.

"You called this meeting, sir."

"Indeed, I did. Frankly, I'm not sure where to start. I don't think I've ever met a freshman who declared a major and had three different folders in her file in her first semester."

"What folders, sir?"

He took the top three folders from the pile nearest him. "Let's see, your student personnel record, with a list of publications already, police reports on two fights with other students and one with a teaching assistant, and a formal proposal to the Curriculum Committee of the College. I'm impressed – no, I'm stunned. " He put two folders back on the desk. "Shall we do the easy one first? Your curriculum vitae. You didn't call it a resumé."

"My parents are researchers, sir. Academic writing is dinner conversation in our house."

"Your publications include articles and short stories in three national magazines. Laudable, but not scholarly research."

"No, but they are relevant to a student of literature and creative writing, are they not?"

"Yes, but I was still surprised. I also did not connect the 'K. Millbank' in *The Daily Free Press* with you until Larry Steinmetz pointed it out. Congratulations."

"Thank you, sir."

A knock on the door preceded Maria's entry with a tray. She set it on a tiny, cleared area on the conference table, then withdrew. He crossed the room and poured two mugs from the carafe. When he sat, he exchanged the personnel folder for the next one.

"About the police reports. In one semester, three calls to 911 involved you. Yet you were never arrested or charged. Explain, please?"

"There were no fights, sir. Each involved a repeated sexual assault after I warned them. I used minimum force to end the assault. All in accordance with the University's sexual harassment policy."

"Just so you know, I helped write that policy. From what I can see in the reports, you followed it to the letter. You walked away, but the others needed medical treatment. Are you a magnet for bad boys?"

"I don't think so, sir. My neighbors in the dorm tell me that I don't get as much harassment as they do. Those reports don't include the wandering hands that don't come back after a warning."

"Okay. Enough on that." He took the last folder from the desk. The main reason I want to talk to you is this. A full-blown proposal for a new undergraduate English curriculum? What are you thinking?"

"It's just the first draft, sir, but I did have to assemble all my facts to pull that much together."

"How long have you had this idea?"

"Since last summer, when I noticed the dearth of women in the required reading lists."

"Did you know that I have been working on this?"

"Not at first, but I came across the article you wrote when you were at Northampton, and I read your dissertation. It came up in a library search."

"You and my dissertation committee may be the only people who have ever read that."

"No, sir. There were twenty-four names on the library checkout card before mine." She smiled. "Was that poll in class related to your research?"

"No. The point was for them to be aware when they read." He waved the proposal. "However, as you note in here, half of the hundred thousand published writers today are women. For our purpose, which is to teach English, we need to identify the best writers for our students to learn from." He extracted a thick typewritten manuscript from the folder and laid the folder back on the pile. "I am humbled, Miss Millbank. Your methodology for this proposal is brilliant. I still have not articulated a convincing way to put forward one particular woman over the others to assemble a recommended list." He held it up to her, then opened it to the abstract in the front. "Explain to me again how you selected your list—with which, by the way, I am in almost complete agreement."

"Quantitative research for a first cut. I posed questions that could be answered by computer searches. I put those to the various libraries that had databases with that information, such as the Widener across the river, and the Library of Congress. Our library here has access to them. I only needed to formulate the questions for the research librarians. As the names came back, it became clear quickly who the great lights were, especially from the nineteenth century."

"I see that. You have provided a list of two dozen women, as well as an appendix, from which the Curriculum Committee could pick other names. It was gutsy to suggest a list of men who should be excluded."

"Not excluded, sir. I recommend creating an optional list, which would include the men transferred from the mandatory reading list and a like number of women. Perhaps only motivated students would dig into those, but one could not say that we kicked out perfectly good authors."

"You seem to have a different criterion working on the twentieth century."

"Yes, sir. As you noted, there are thousands of published writers now, so I was out of my depth almost right away. How could I determine who was just fun to read, compared to who could teach me how to write better or to think critically? So, I took a stab at all three. I'm sure the Committee will take issue with my choices, but that is why I have provided many more twentieth-century names in the appendices."

"I circled a few names that strike me as strange." He handed her the proposal. "Why Garnett, Hays, and Ashurst? They're translators, not writers. And Sayers? Are you a Peter Wimsey fan?"

"Not really. I learned from one of my mother's friends that translators are first of all writers in the target language, and those four exemplify that. Without Weavers' English, would *The Name of the Rose* ever have become the global best-seller that it is? Sayers gave us *The Divine Comedy* in a colloquial English that laypersons can understand and enjoy. And who wrote George Sand in English? Matilda Hays and Elizabeth Ashurst. Whatever Russian scholars may think of her translations, Constance Garnett brought Russian literature to the English-speaking world and made Dostoyevsky a best-selling author. Today, there are entire departments of Russian that would not have been created had it not been for her."

"Where did you learn all this?"

"My parents did not send me to my room when entertaining their colleagues. With one parent in medicine and the other in the humanities, I was doomed." He snorted at that. "They also played devil's advocate to any hare-brained idea I came up with. It was hard to pout and stomp away when they argued with me. They made me stay until either I or they had convinced the other. Usually, we compromised."

"Remarkable parents. I would like to meet them."

"My mother's family lives near Cape Ann. They'll be back, sir."

***

The brilliant green of spring yielded slowly to a darker green heading towards summer. Running along the Charles River, Katherine and her two friends could smell flowers between the clouds of automobile exhaust coming from Storrow Drive.

Katherine was glad that she had decided to drop the track team. She enjoyed running with Rosie and Laura. The two women repeatedly thanked her for keeping them in shape, which made her happier than fame on the track would have. The three of them also met every Saturday for their mini triathlon that ended at the natatorium.

Back at Shelton Hall, she found a note from the resident assistant taped to their door. "K – Please call Prof. Ardmore ASAP."

"And I was just about to ask you how the proposal was going," said Laura.

"So far, great. There was no pushback from the department. It should be with the Dean of the College this week."

The door swung shut behind them. Katherine unlocked the drawer where they kept the cellular bag phone and called the department office.

"Hello, Maria. I got a note from Professor Ardmore to call him ASAP. Is there a problem?"

"He's with the Dean right now. When he gets back, I'm sure he'll want to see you. Can you come over?"

"I need a shower, but I'll be over right away. Is it about the proposal?"

"That's not the only thing he sees the Dean about, but your proposal probably did come up. I'll tell him you're coming if he beats you here."

Twenty minutes later, Katherine sat in Maria's office, reviewing her copy of the proposal, and sipping water from the Anselmo Aces bicycle bottle that she carried almost everywhere. She had just made some notes in the references, which she needed to check for her journal article, when the chairman walked in.

"Katherine! Come in, please."

Maria mouthed "Katherine" with arched eyebrows and a grin behind his back. Katherine shrugged and followed him in. He moved swiftly to his desk, which was clean and tidy now, and sat in his chair. He motioned for her to sit.

"Sorry about that slip in decorum. I am so excited about your proposal and the progress it's made, that I stopped referring to you as Miss Millbank in private. I hope you don't mind."

"No, sir. That's fine." She paused. "But I hope you don't want me to Reggie you in public." She smiled while he laughed.

"Touché. No. And I'll watch myself outside this office." He put the folder on the desk. "We've hit our first obstacle. The Dean tried to tell me that a student can't make proposals for curriculum changes. After I argued down all his procedural objections, he said some garbage about degrading the quality of the students who go on to the graduate programs.

"I'm afraid it got a little heated – at least as heated as it can get without his throwing me out of the office. I told him that I would be back."

"What now, sir?"

"I go back—now. But I want you to come with me."

"Sir?" Katherine suppressed a gasp and felt her head spin. The last thing she expected was to be confronting a dean as a freshman. *This is worse than seeing the high school principal,* she thought. Ardmore was looking at her with a gentle smile on his face. His eyes were a little wide, hopeful maybe. *Or would it be worse?*

"What do you know about our exalted dean?"

"His field is linguistic anthropology. Degrees from New York University, Italy, and Princeton. He came here from the University of Minnesota. His publications center on Native American languages."

Ardmore's jaw dropped. He pulled it up and blushed. "Of course, you would have researched everyone in the chain of approval. Right?"

"Yes, sir. What is his objection?"

"Frankly, Katherine, I don't think he has one. He's just old-fashioned enough not to want to entertain the idea. However, despite his attitude, he is a first-rate scholar; he would accept a frank exchange of ideas. You are a walking surprise to most of the faculty here. He just hasn't met you."

"If his mind is made up, what could I do?"

"Change it. He can only oppose you with well-founded reasons, not just because he said so. Do you know what a colloquium is?"

"Of course. I attended several when my mother or father was presenting."

"I suspected as much. I think the meeting will quickly turn into that sort of confrontation, and I don't expect that he is ready to go up against you that way."

"You're scaring me, sir."

"Sorry, but I don't think he'll be able to justify resisting the proposal after he meets you. He has always shown respect for well-formed arguments, enjoys them even. And that includes arguments from the women in the College. Let him play the devil's advocate; he won't hurt you or resent you."

"Well, okay, sir. Do we go now?"

"Yes." He checked his watch. "I was so confident about this, that I made an appointment with his secretary on my way out. Let's go." He gathered the proposal and marched out. Katherine followed him, shaking her head.

The dean was not Italian, but the bright kid from Brooklyn *had* won a Fulbright scholarship to La Sapienza University in Rome. Shorter than Katherine, with a round face, black hair and moustache going grey, and brown eyes magnified by his thick glasses. His eyes turned even bigger when Katherine came in behind Professor Ardmore.

"Reginald, you have brought the author?"

"Federico Manzoni, this is Katherine Millbank, an English major in the College."

"You told me that an undergraduate wrote the proposal, but I expected someone older, perhaps a senior. How old are you, dear?"

Katherine bristled, and clenched her teeth, hoping not to show it. The words of her grandmother came back to her, "Don't dally around. Take the initiative."

"Is my age or sex relevant, sir? I am quite prepared to discuss the content of the proposal with you. And since I have been closer to it than anyone else, I can probably answer all your questions."

Manzoni stood back as if he had been slapped. He recovered quickly and motioned to the conference table.

"Where are my manners? Please, let's sit." After calling out for coffee, he sat at the head of the table with Katherine and Professor Ardmore on either side.

For the next hour, the dean asked questions ranging from how and why Katherine got the idea for the proposal to the specific contributions that the women would make to the students' store of knowledge. He challenged each of the two dozen men moved to the appendix. Sweat was trickling between her breasts as Katherine revealed which women offered a richer perspective than the men they replaced on the mandatory list, and the additional perspectives that they brought to the study.

He quizzed her carefully to understand how she sorted the results of the first computer runs to determine who was a model for better writing, who challenged the reader to think, and who exemplified excellent writing that held the student's interest.

Katherine listed the specific scholars who had written on the points she was making in the proposal. Manzoni found himself looking at Ardmore more and more often, when Katherine's sources and the depth of her answers passed beyond his own previous experience.

Including the four translators surprised him, but he acknowledged that exposing the students to the role of translation in bringing foreign literature to them and learning from the translators' use of English was a win-win.

"This could give a boost to our language departments, considering how much of their material is taught in translation," Manzoni said. "I like it."

Fifteen minutes later, he closed his copy of the proposal.

"Miss Millbank, I am amazed, but I concede that this has been an enthralling experience. It makes our Friday afternoon colloquia feel boring. Thank you."

"Will you approve it?"

"No, I won't." He paused to watch Katherine's face fall, then chuckled. "That is up to the Faculty of the College. But the Curriculum Committee will be meeting tomorrow, and I was the last–and probably the heaviest–holdout." He glanced at the grinning Ardmore. "Not a word, Reginald!"

He stood and shook their hands. He walked to the door and held it for them.

On their way back to the English department, Ardmore told Katherine that the provost was already looking forward to the proposal.

"Before today, I was optimistic. Now I'm confident." He stopped outside his office. "Well done, Katherine. Well done indeed."

***

Two weeks before the final Reading Days, Katherine asked for an appointment with the chairman. The new Mr. Coffee machine had just finished sputtering when she entered the office. He set her mug on the conference table and motioned to the chair.

"This time you called the meeting, Katherine."

"Yes, sir. I was not sure about this, but your support of the proposal makes me want to show it to you."

"Another proposal?"

"No, sir. An article for *College English.* It takes my research for the proposal and provides the reader a process for building balance into their curriculum."

"Why am I not surprised? I was thinking of such an article myself, but I thought to have the proposal accepted first."

"My idea was to publish the research first. It can't hurt to have that kind of support for the proposal, can it?"

Ardmore sipped his coffee while he paged through the manuscript.

"My goodness, young lady, you are turning into quite the scholar. May I keep this?"

"I made that copy for you. I won't submit it until after final exams, and I would welcome any suggestions. I also gave it to the TA in charge of my section."

"Larry Steinmetz."

"Yes, sir."

"He's a fan, you know."

"No, I didn't, but he has been supportive, and a ruthless editor, for which I am grateful."

"Thank you for giving me some time with it. I'll get back to you."

Katherine stood. "Thank you, sir."

"Thank *you.* If they publish this, it will be a win for everyone: here, and in other schools."

***

Katherine paused in the air conditioning at Logan Airport departures to unstick her blouse from her wet chest. The last few weeks had featured mad dashes every day. Professor Ardmore came back five times to ask her about changes to the proposal, as various committee members up the line tried to impress their superiors in meetings.

Just two days before final exams, he told her that the proposal would probably be acted on during the summer. He said there was barely enough time to change all the catalogs and course descriptions.

"It may have to wait for next year, but that would allow us to work on the various documents and publications more calmly. Just think of the strain on the teachers to choose new texts for their courses." He grinned. "When you come back you will either have a ticker tape parade or be burned at the stake by an angry mob. Enjoy your summer."

She had put the manuscript to *College English* in the mail on her way to Logan. Laura would check the mail for them both during the summer. Not that anyone expected an answer before September.

***

The phone rang in the entrance hall. Katherine heard her mother answer as she walked down the stairs.

"No, this is Louise Millbank." Mother glanced at daughter. "However, Katherine is here. Just a moment..." She handed the handset to her daughter.

"Hello. This is Katherine Millbank."

"Miss Millbank, this is Peter Williams."

"*College English.*" Katherine stifled a gasp. She controlled her voice as best she could. "What can I do for you, sir?"

"That's the first time someone I did not know recognized my name."

"I've seen it in enough issues."

"Oh, right. Anyway, I called about the article you submitted in early June. The submission form states your affiliation as "Boston University," but not the faculty position. Are you in a tenured or tenure-track position?"

"No, sir. Is it relevant? I understood that the reviews would be blind."

"Not really, but I've read a lot of research on English curricula, as you can imagine, and the depth and direction of yours made me wonder where I know you from. I could not find you in the faculty directory at BU or the nearby schools. I even checked the Boston phone book."

"I'm an English major, sir."

"An undergraduate?"

"Yes, sir."

"And who made the proposal that BU is implementing next year?" Katherine held back a squeak. *The president must have signed it!*

"I did, sir, although Professor Ardmore, our department chair, did the heavy lifting through the various committees."

"Does he know you submitted this article?"

"Oh, yes, sir. I showed it to him after submitting the curriculum change proposal. He made some helpful suggestions before I sent it to you."

"Why isn't he a co-author?"

"I asked him about that, and he said that he did not contribute enough to the research to deserve it. Do I need a faculty co-author, sir? That is not spelled out in the guidelines."

After a brief silence, Williams said, "No, not really. But do you mind if I talk to him about it before I decide whether to send it to peer review?"

"No, sir."

"Thank you. I'll talk to him myself to keep this confidential. We'll notify you of the steps by mail, of course." He verified her mailing address, then hung up.

***

Shredding trails in the Samuel Taylor State Park, swimming in the Pacific, and riding to see her friends kept Katherine busy and happy. She returned to Massachusetts in mid-August, tanned and rested. With her grandmother, she enjoyed hiking the trails around Essex County, and long conversations about their family history. They spoke in Pawtucket most of the time, as Katherine's ease with the language grew.

A letter from *College English* was in her student mailbox. Peter Williams thanked her for the manuscript and reported that it was in peer review. She should not expect a decision before Christmas.

She spent her sophomore year excelling in her studies—when she wasn't writing historical fiction for magazines, running with her friends, or riding her bicycle. The article in the Spring issue of *College English* made her something of a celebrity in the English Department and the College.

Larry Steinmetz defended his dissertation and took a job at Boston College nearby. Katherine dated him and a student librarian she met at the Widener Library.

By the time she graduated, Katherine Millbank was publishing fiction and non-fiction regularly. Her plan to study overlooked contributions of women in medicine figured in the university's decision to offer her a scholarship to fund her master's degree. She began running marathons and triathlons, meeting interesting men and women, and satisfying her competitive drive to race.

The men she met running were smart, fit, and fun to be with. Only one became a problem, but that is a different story for another time.

CHARLIE

KATHERINE MILLBANK picked up a bean bag paperweight from the desk and tossed it gently at the sleeping lump across the room.

"Up and at 'em, sleepyhead!"

The form groaned into her pillow. "Wha' time zit?"

"Six-thirty. Starting gun at eight."

"Why did I ever get into this?" Sarah Franciano threw back the covers and sat on the edge of the bed, her elbows on her knees. Her sandy blonde hair fell over her face.

"You mean, why did you let Scotty take you to a party on a Friday night?"

"That, too." Sarah looked up, suddenly wide awake. "I'll bet he feels worse than I do!"

"Coffee's made. I'll put out some breakfast." Katherine closed the door on her housemate and padded back to the kitchen in her slippers.

The two women had shared the apartment in Foggy Bottom for two years. Katherine was pursuing a doctorate in English Literature, but already had published journal articles on little-known women of the eighteenth and nineteenth centuries who were writing ahead of their times. Sarah would finish her master's in teaching about the same time Katherine expected to defend her dissertation. They had met in the waiting lounge of the off-campus housing referral office and quickly discovered their shared passion for triathlons and teaching. Sarah was three years older, having taught for a while before returning to graduate school. Katherine had taught part-time while pursuing her master's at Boston University. When the George Washington University made her an offer, she jumped at it. Now they were in the last semester of their studies and their lease.

As Sarah came into the kitchen, Katherine put out two bowls of muesli, a tub of yogurt and a bowl of fruit.

"You clean up pretty good," said Katherine.

"Not so loud. My stomach might hear you!"

"Here. Drink this first. You need some water in you."

"I know. Why didn't I remember to drink more water last night?"

"You *do* get distracted when Scotty is around." Katherine grinned. "Isn't he running, too?"

"Yeah. I may come in next to last, instead of dead last."

They ate their breakfast mostly in silence. Sarah recovered quickly, as young athletes in top form can do. By the time they jogged to Dupont Circle for the start of the amateur half-marathon, both women were ready to race.

Sarah and Katherine competed in the triathlon circuit on the East Coast. They used amateur events like this half-marathon as training days and to socialize. This race was a fundraiser for the League of Women Voters, a cause close to Katherine's heart. Considered a warm-up for the large marathons later in the year, it attracted both the sports media and the political press.

The air felt cool and fresh as the athletes gathered at the starting line. The sun was just clearing the lower buildings around Dupont Circle when the starting gun sent two thousand women and men running up Connecticut Avenue. Katherine immediately set into her cruising pace, not feeling like showing off. She found a position just behind a half dozen men she recognized from the Marine Corps Marathon the year before. Running in what looked like the pack, she did not attract attention by being so far ahead of the next woman in the race.

She only sensed the presence of other runners around her, avoiding elbows as easily as road hazards, and using almost invisible spurts of speed to keep her position. Sarah ran with the first group of women. After running uphill on Connecticut Avenue, then down Nebraska to Georgetown, the race made its way to the National Mall.

The pack had thinned out considerably by the time the lead group turned onto Constitution Avenue for the last mile to the Capitol Building. Katherine moved up to fourth place, causing the first six men to glance at her quickly and begin sprinting, perhaps too early for most of them. Her friend Bahari from Kenya never looked back, but she knew that he knew who was behind him, including her. She admired his incredibly long legs as he flowed effortlessly over the asphalt. She did not consider that observers on the sidelines might think that she and Bahari were dancing, their strides being so well matched.

Easing up behind Bahari, Katherine found herself next to a runner she had never seen before. Pale, clean-shaven, maybe late twenties, dark brown hair, cut very short, he looked more like a swimmer than a runner.

Another triathlete, she thought. As she prepared to sprint with Bahari for the finish, the new guy surprised her by falling into step with the two of them. Soon the three were running side-by-side. The others fell ten or more meters behind.

As they tore through the tape, each of them grabbed a piece of it. Bahari won the photo-finish, but a tie was ruled for second place. Maury Cavendish, an Irish junior diplomat, won third place.

At the podium, the race officials suffered a moment of distress in front of the press and the crowd (this was an amateur race, after all). They had extra medals, but only three positions on the podium.

"Get up there," Katherine said, pushing the stranger to the block. "I've seen the view already."

The man's face was beet-red, as he mounted the podium with Bahari and Maury, and smiled for the photos. "Thanks," he said. Katherine stepped back.

He was still trying to get down from the podium when the crowd of reporters surrounded Katherine, taking pictures and shouting questions. She smiled and gave her usual non-committal answers–and swore once again to herself that she was going to give this up somehow. But she knew she could never stop competing—she loved it too much. She just wished the press weren't there. She missed the single-track races in the Samuel Taylor State Park, where nobody saw the finish but the judges and the racers' families.

As soon as she could, Katherine slipped into the crowd of runners stretching near the finish and found Sarah.

"How'd it go?" Katherine asked as she bent down to stretch her back and glutes.

"Not bad. Third woman, twenty-seventh overall. I can see you were out there, as usual."

"Yeah, well, I like hanging out with Bahari. He's so shy that I'm going to have to ask him for a date next time." They laughed.

"Who's the new guy?"

"I don't know. Number 1307. We can look it up."

"Look it up? Katherine, he's hot! You didn't introduce yourself?"

"Oh, yeah. I don't feel like getting acquainted here. Remember the article in *Sports Illustrated*? That was disgusting. I felt like a piece of meat."

"Okay. Let's get out of here. You obviously are not ready for the celebrity pages."

"Hey, where's Scotty?"

"He had to go the john after he finished his paperwork. He'll meet us at the Metro."

They pushed further into the crowd and made their way to the subway below Union Station. Most of the runners had family, friends, or agents picking them up at the finish, but the three of them found that it was easier to get home on their own when they were ready.

Stepping off the escalator onto the platform for the Red Line, Sarah grabbed Katherine's arm. "There's Scotty! C'mon." Katherine stopped suddenly, causing Sarah to stumble.

"That's the new guy."

Scotty spotted them and waved them over. He gave Sarah an affectionate hug.

"You two did well, I see." He pulled the man closer. "Sarah, this is Charlie Hampstead. You two met already, I guess."

Charlie and Sarah shook hands, but Charlie stared at Katherine. "We haven't met, actually." He smiled broadly. His handshake was firm and warm.

"Katherine Millbank. I'm Sarah's housemate."

"Not Kathy or Kate?"

"Please, no. Katherine."

"I was stunned when you made me get on the podium. You won that spot."

"Like I said, I've been there. You're a top runner to pace Bahari like that. Why haven't we seen you before?"

"I only came to DC last week."

"Charlie's a Marine and my best friend."

Sarah pouted, but her eyes twinkled. "I thought I was your best friend."

"Sure, as long as Charlie was chasing bad guys overseas. Now he's my best guy friend. Okay?" He held his hand up for a high-five.

"Okay."

"Here's our train."

They gathered at one end of the car, a happy, sweaty foursome. Charlie was staying with Scotty while he looked for his own place. He was stationed at Eighth and Eye, the Marine Corps base in Southeast Washington.

They got off at Dupont Circle and walked to the coffee shop at the corner of New Hampshire Avenue. The server smiled when she saw them.

"One of these days, we gotta install a locker room with showers. Over there." She waved at a corner booth with the coffee carafe. "Be right with you."

"Thanks, Rosalie."

After they ordered and started their coffees, Katherine noticed Charlie looking at her with a quizzical look. She suddenly realized that she had been staring at him.

"Sorry. I zoned out there." She blinked and sipped her coffee. "So, what do you do at—what is it? —Eighth and Eye?" Charlie smiled.

"Nothing. I have to go in each day for some processing, but mostly it's waiting around."

"Is that normal?"

"No. My unit was ordered here suddenly, so everyone is in limbo."

Katherine arched her eyebrows for him to continue, but he looked at his coffee.

"Later, Katherine," said Scotty. "It hasn't been a picnic."

"Sorry. I've been told that I'm too curious. Please forgive me."

Charlie looked up. "Nothing to forgive." He smiled warmly. "Think we can take Scotty up on that word?"

"Which word?"

"'Later.' I would like to see you again, even though I've only seen you run. I know nothing else about you."

Sarah and Scotty laughed. Katherine sat back, a little shocked.

"Well, why not?" She blinked. "Are you asking me on a date already?"

"I don't have my calendar in my running shorts. May I call you?"

Scotty and Sarah finally calmed down.

"Katherine, I knew you were fast, but that's a record, girl."

Their food arrived, and they concentrated on replacing their carbs and proteins.

****

Seeing Charlie again proved easier than she expected. He called the next day, and they arranged to meet at the library after her Monday seminar. They walked to O Street for lunch.

Over a large, four-cheese pizza, they exchanged the usual background information. He grew up in Oregon. His parents were both teachers. After graduating from the Naval Academy, he had served in Iraq, Hawaii, and Okinawa. He enjoyed racing in triathlons. Scotty had told him about the half-marathon, so he signed up. She grew up in Marin County in California when the mountain bike racing craze was exploding. In college, she found women's sports too tame, so she turned to triathlons and marathons to feed her competitive drive.

He was fascinated by her athletic accomplishments but seemed even more impressed by her scholarship. At one point, he looked out the window, as a sadness came over his face.

"I don't know much about feminism or literature, being a dumb jarhead," he said, turning to face her, "but I do know one thing. The world would be a better place with the women in charge."

"That's a strong statement for a Marine, isn't it?"

"It applies especially to the Corps. It's partly why I'm resigning."

"Oh. So, this is not a routine reassignment?"

Charlie looked down, toyed with his pizza slice, then drank some water. He sighed and looked up at her.

"No. My whole unit was brought back. I'm the CO." He paused, as if trying to make up his mind. Katherine kept quiet. "Maybe later, I'll be able to tell you about it."

He took a bite of his pizza and switched the subject. He had been a varsity swimmer at the Naval Academy, and like everyone else, ran every day. Adding the cycling was easy as triathlons caught on at Marine bases and their local communities. While he was stationed at Kaneohe on Oahu, he signed up for the Iron Man Triathlon. He had usually come in first before, but he placed in the early part of the pack in that one. So it was for any big event where people came from far away.

"I seem to catch up on each leg, but the transitions just kill me. I don't know how the pros can change so fast."

"Kind of hard to spy on the competition when they're changing in and out of swimsuits in a tent, isn't it?" He nodded. "We can work on that, if you want." He raised his eyebrows.

"Are you offering to help me strip and dress?" Katherine gasped lightly.

"Oh my gosh, did I say that?" They both laughed. "You know what I mean!"

"How did you go from mountain biking to triathlons?" He listened intently as Katherine described the scenes in Fort Bragg, California, and Boston. They chatted easily until Katherine had to leave for an afternoon meeting with her advisor.

***

They met for a movie the next night, which brought the first sort-of-argument in their 24-hour relationship. They were nearing the end of supper at a casual restaurant near the theater.

"Thanks for lunch yesterday, but I'd rather pay my own way. Don't go all gentleman on me."

Charlie looked hurt, "But—" Then he shut his mouth, staring into her narrowed eyes as he considered what she really meant. "I get it but look at it this way. I've got the nice government job, and you're a grad student making ends meet. Let me pay the bill. I could be unemployed and homeless next month. What do you say?"

Katherine took a breath as if to argue, then held it, and let it out. "Okay. But let me get the movie tickets."

"Deal." He reached out his hand and they shook. She smiled and squeezed his hand rather longer than a casual gesture. "If you want to keep seeing me, let's take turns paying. This way, the waitstaff doesn't have to split the bill."

"Okay." she said. "And the one who doesn't pay leaves the tip."

***

Later, neither could remember which movie they went to that night, because "dinner and a movie" became a pleasant frequent experience for them. Katherine noticed that when it was his turn, he chose the more expensive places and suggested the more casual ones for her to pay. Charlie would often meet her between classes. On the third day after first meeting, he and Scotty ran into Sarah and Katherine running in the morning. The four friends started running every morning after that. On the weekends, they swam at the university pool and cycled on the bike paths that started at Rock Creek and ran into Virginia and Maryland.

One evening when it was Charlie's turn to pay, Katherine asked, "You seem very quiet tonight. Is everything okay?" He sighed.

"Sorry it shows. Sometimes it just gets me down."

"Want to tell me about it? I only know that you're a Marine officer, so I guess you can't let weakness show at work or something like that, eh?"

He gazed off beyond her shoulder as if gathering his thoughts. The flickering of the candle on the table made his hazel eyes shift color rapidly between green and brown. Katherine stared until he blinked.

"Remember what I said about how I wish the women were in charge?"

"Yes."

"Half the Marines in my unit are women. We've deployed twice together, and the respect we have for one another is total and unconditional. From the beginning, the women have been solid Marines like the men. Some of the guys started out being a little fatherly in their concern for the women—until they got slapped in the head or found themselves on the ground with a combat boot poised over their balls. The first deployment was a learning experience for everyone." He smiled.

Katherine grinned. "I take it you had to be the teacher?" He nodded.

"We were back at our main base after the second deployment. It can get pretty boring between deployments, so we never get any slack at home. One night, we got a call to a local club, where a private party had turned into a drunken bash. The responders called for backup, so I took the rest of the duty section to the club. We found two squads gang-banging a half-dozen women: four of their own Marines and a pair of locals. Everyone was wild-eyed, but it was clear that the women were not having fun. Their platoon commander, a brand-new second lieutenant, had passed out under a table. We arrested him and the twenty men and took the women to the base clinic for rape kits, counseling, and interrogation."

Katherine gasped and forced herself not to talk. She motioned for Charlie to continue.

"It would have been a major scandal, so the major—my boss—did not want it getting out. But I was not going to tolerate sexual assault."

"You said 'arrested.' Are you some kind of policeman?"

"Security Battalion. What the Army calls military police."

"What happened?"

"I was ordered to withdraw the charges while the platoon was reassigned. The brass wanted to cover it up. They said everyone was having fun."

"And?"

"I refused. So did my whole unit, even the ones who were not part of the original arrest. The local JAG officers—that's the Judge Advocate General corps, the lawyers—warned the command that the men were duly arrested and charged. One by one, they relieved us of our duties, until there was no one left to withdraw the charges. They flew us to Washington, reassigned everyone they could, and threatened to court-martial the rest of us for insubordination."

"You're kidding."

"No. But it can't stick, so they're in a bind—all the way to the top. They hushed it up, but now they have a dozen Marines they don't know what to do with—and a whole chain of command ready to collapse with the next scandal. I'm disgusted." He paused to take a breath. "I don't care if it started out as drunken fun. When I got there, the women were screaming and terrified. It was rape, pure and simple."

"Is this like that Tailhook scandal in Las Vegas?"

"Worse. They were raping their own Marines and local women."

Katherine felt the steak burn in her stomach. She took a deep breath and stared at him.

"Why are you sharing this with me? We only just met."

"Because I think you'll understand. I don't know anyone else who would, except the men and women in my unit."

"Scotty is your friend."

"He's supportive, but he doesn't get it."

"Really, no one?"

"Not my parents, not the chaplain, and certainly no other Marines."

"What do they say?"

"Different things, but behind it all, they point out that the women were drunk. As if the men weren't or that it's okay for the men to be drunk but not the women."

"I've heard that: blame the victim."

"When you explained your work, I thought you might."

Katherine reached over and took his hand. "I'm very sorry. But I'm also impressed by your courage."

"I don't feel so courageous right now, unloading my troubles on you."

"To the people in your unit, you must be a hero."

"They're taking it pretty hard."

"But are they regretting it?"

"Not that I can tell."

"So, it's your unit against the whole male supremacy system in the Marine Corps."

"Pretty much."

"It's good that you have each other. It sounds very scary." She sipped her wine. "What will you do now?"

"Right now, I have to win the fight to make sure my Marines get their honorable discharges. The JAG officers have been great, keeping the Corps from kicking them all out with dishonorable discharges. I told them not to settle for general discharges. But it takes time. Eventually, though, they'll have to let them all go honorably, or it won't be a quiet discharge."

"What about you?"

"I'll resign my commission and take an honorable discharge like the others. I've met my minimum service obligation, so they can't keep me."

"It seems sad."

"I loved the Corps. We all did. This feels like the worst betrayal—to be taught a set of principles, then watch everyone blow them off."

"And after the Corps?"

"I haven't gotten there yet. Probably graduate school on the GI Bill. I don't worry about being unemployed with my resumé."

"Tough, but it seems that you'll be okay in the end."

"Yes, we will." He took a breath and a sip of his wine. "Thanks."

"What for?"

"Listening. I've never been able to get all this out at once like this. Once I did, I realized that it's not as bad as it feels. We really can get through this."

"You're welcome, then. Please let me know how it's going. This is the most amazing story. I want to organize something, but that would ruin what you are trying to do, wouldn't it?"

"Yes."

"It just makes me so mad to see the brass getting away with this. They need to be exposed."

Charlie squeezed her hand. "They're not getting away with anything. This will come out someday and bite them badly. But my first duty is to my Marines. Always. I have to see them safely out of this mess, so they can get on with their lives. You see?"

Katherine nodded. They sat back and looked at each other for a while. The server approached the table.

"Want me to box that for you?"

The question surprised Katherine. Charlie was looking at her to see what she wanted, too.

"Actually, not yet. I'm still hungry. Sorry."

"That's okay." The server put a fresh carafe of water on the table and left.

Charlie smiled and attacked his steak. "Heavy talk. I forgot that I came in here hungry."

"Me, too."

***

Two weeks later, Sarah came home and stood in the door to Katherine's room.

"Charlie wasn't home tonight. I thought he'd be out with you."

Katherine hit the ENTER key and stood up. "Me, too." She stretched and turned to her friend. "He's having a farewell party of sorts with his unit. They got their discharges today and processed out."

"All at once?"

"Yes. And Charlie has lined up jobs for all of them." Katherine counted off. "Let's see. Six are joining police departments in their hometowns, four have accepted offers from security or investigations companies, and two are going to college: one to Howard and the other to Sweet Briar, on a combination of GI Bill and scholarships."

"Wow!"

"Turns out he can write a pretty powerful recommendation letter. Not your usual form reference."

"No wonder they stuck by him. What about Charlie himself?"

"He submitted his letter of resignation. It may take a while for it to be accepted, because the people who sign off on it are scared shitless. But he has his JAG friends standing by. Charlie thinks that they'll let him go if they think he'll go quietly."

"You've been seeing him almost every day. Are you two an item?"

"Gosh, I haven't thought about it. I like being with him, and he seems to enjoy being with me. I don't have many people who understand me, and he seems to have the same problem."

"Well, if you want to bring that puppy home with you, just let me know, because right now, I'm not spending nights at Scotty's, you know."

"Yeah, right. That would be nice." Katherine walked to the kitchen for another glass of juice. The prospect of more than good-night kisses with Charlie made her smile.

Sarah called down the hall, "Scotty said that he and Charlie won't run tomorrow. What time do you want to go?" asked Sarah.

"I want to finish the draft on this chapter, so I may sleep in. Say, eight o'clock?"

"Okay. Good night, Katherine."

"Good night, Sarah. And thanks."

THE NEXT GENERATION ARRIVES

A LEAD BASKETBALL, she thought. *Is there any round thing heavier than that?* Katherine Hampstead took another deep breath and rose to her feet from the hard plastic chair. While Charlie pulled their luggage from the carousel, she walked across the baggage claim area to get her suitcase. The ache in her back had eased with the short rest sitting.

"Let me get that, honey."

Katherine gave him *that look.* "You can get the rest of them, macho man."

"I get it. Just don't be a hero on me. I'd much rather have her born at the GW hospital than the San Francisco airport."

Katherine smiled, which made him smile, too. She loved his smiling face almost more than any sight she could think of.

"She hasn't even dropped yet. Don't worry."

"How you can even walk straight with that load, I'll never understand."

"No, you never will." She patted his back. "Be grateful for the small favors of your sex." She motioned with her head to her parents coming out of the crowd by the door. "There they are."

People often mistook Katherine and her mother for sisters. Auburn hair, high cheekbones, and hazel eyes. Something about the genes in generations of survivors had given them both exceptional strength and endurance. Even the worst life experiences had failed to diminish them.

Louise Massey and Martin Millbank had met at the battle for Khe Sanh in Vietnam; he a young surgeon, she a combat nurse in the field operating station. They were both wounded but chose not to be evacuated during the fighting. When their tours were completed, they transferred back to California together. They were wed the day after they took their discharges. Martin accepted a position at Tufts University Medical Center in Boston. The GI Bill of Rights put Louise through graduate school. By the time Katherine was born, Louise's career as a linguistic anthropologist was gaining traction.

Martin took the suitcase from Katherine, who immediately relieved Charlie of one of the cases he was pulling. Louise smiled and winked at her daughter. Long ago, she had learned to appreciate Katherine's strong spirit.

The humid heat hit them like a wall of water. The Bay Area was famous for not having extremes of weather, but this summer was exceptional, and the chill of the air-conditioned airport amplified the shock. Katherine was sweating freely by the time they piled into the car and found Highway 101 north to Marin County.

For six days, the Millbanks and the Hampsteads sorted, removed, donated, packed, and shipped personal items. Martin had announced his retirement a year ago, and they had worked hard to downsize to the last few essentials. At the end of the week, an estate auctioneer and her crew came to the house and efficiently carried out every remaining piece of furniture and household goods in the house. She would send them the proceeds of the auction later.

Wendy Marburg, who had been Katherine's best friend in school, put them up for the last night. The three couples ate out that night.

"It feels real now, Mom," said Katherine after they ordered at the restaurant. "I can't believe we watched twenty years vanish so fast."

"We've been organizing this for a year," said Louise, "but it is still a shock to take the final steps."

"And we've been back to Massachusetts three times this year," said Martin. "Your grandmother is ready for us."

"Are you ready to walk as much as she does?" At ninety years old, Marian Massey still walked everywhere within a five-mile radius from her home in the Great Marsh North Wildlife Management Area.

"Sure, but all those cousins, nieces, and nephews have been falling over themselves to drive us around. With the T right there in Rowley, we can take the train to Newburyport, Ipswich, or Boston."

The next morning, the Purple Heart Association people showed up to take possession of Martin's old car (a tax-deductible donation), and the real estate agent arrived to inspect the house and take the keys. By four p.m., Wendy had left them at the departures area at San Francisco airport for the next chapter of their lives.

***

Katherine spotted Marian Massey's silver hair above the crowd as they walked into the baggage claim area at Logan International Airport. It was tied back in a long braid, as Katherine had always remembered it. Maybe a few more lines on the tanned face, but her grandmother stood as erect and solid as ever. Katherine ran to the matriarch and hugged her tightly.

"Goodness, girl. You need longer arms!"

"She's all Massey, Nigå. Kicking like a street fighter."

With hugs exchanged, including cousin John Harwich, the family walked to the parking area. John was the same age as Katherine. He had been named for her maternal grandfather.

"And how are Niben and the little one?" asked Katherine. "What's her name now?"

"We're calling her *Nolka*, because she's so fast!" Deer. John grinned. "But Niben says she may become *Pitlålo* if she keeps beating up the boys who try to bully her at school." Mountain Lion. The Harwich girl was in first grade.

Katherine and Louise laughed. "That sounds like our family," said Louise. Katherine had been notorious at Drake High School for putting down bullies and protecting the younger girls. "Between now and her coming-of-age ceremony, she'll probably earn several names that could stick."

They loaded into the van that John had brought from work. Marian sat next to him. Louise and Martin behind them, and Katherine and Charlie in the last row. John was a careful driver, patiently waiting behind the harried commuters, as he and Marian talked, with Louise commenting periodically. Katherine tried to pick out as much of the Pawtucket as she could, but mostly she felt the sensation of a babbling brook wash over her. The Western Abenaki language was a gentle tongue, almost a murmuring compared to European languages.

She started awake when Charlie kissed the top of her head. "We're here," he said. "Well, almost."

"Omigod. Did I fall asleep?"

"Yup. I nodded off myself sometimes."

They had stopped at the end of Town Farm Road. Katherine smelled the Ipswich Transfer Station on the southeast breeze. Two large carts with fat tires were parked where the asphalt dropped off. She recognized the carts that her grandmother had built years ago, to haul the trash and recycle bins from her house to the transfer station.

"One cart for the luggage, the other for Katherine," said Marian.

"I'll walk, thank you very much."

"I expected you to say that, *chajigåwa*, but don't be too proud to jump in at any point. And do NOT try to pull it."

"Yes, Nigå. What does chajigåwa mean?"

"Stubborn one." Marian patted Katherine's arm. They smiled at each other as Louise and the three men emptied the luggage from the back of the van.

The proximity of water and the frequent patches of shade as they walked the trail into the marsh did much to abate the heat. Even with the weight of the impatient being inside her, Katherine felt the same delight she remembered the first time she had walked this trail as a rising freshman at Boston University. It had been a memorable summer for all three women in the small party.

Watching her grandmother and mother walking with their heads together, murmuring with relaxing tones of the Pawtucket language, Katherine sighed with pleasure at the thought of her mother outgrowing the anger that had led her to leave this marsh at eighteen and join the Army. She came out of Vietnam with the kind of supportive and equal partner that Pawtucket women favor, but it took her another twenty years to appreciate that fact. Meanwhile, she had pursued Native American languages with a scholarly passion, acquiring Salish and Lakota before recognizing her own roots. While Katherine had pursued her own studies in English literature, Louise had added the Eastern Algonquian languages to her studies, becoming fluent in Western Abenaki and Pawtucket.

Doctor Martin Millbank may have retired, but Doctor Louise Massey was just embarking on a new and exciting phase in her academic career. She did not want the Pawtucket language to die with her mother and her aunts.

Less than a half-hour later, the family was moving into the old house on the edge of the Egypt River near Shad Creek. Marian directed Katherine to the small room that had been Louise's, and then hers while she was in college. Someone had set up a twin bed for Charlie. The guest room would become the Millbanks' new home.

"Goodness, Nigå," said Louise as they carried their suitcases into the guest room. "Who put in the cooktop and counter?"

"Who do you think? Your grandmother and I built the place, after all."

"More than I expected, downsizing from the house in California," said Martin.

"Doing what I can to ease the culture shock." Marian winked. "Between that and the water closet there, this should give you all the privacy you need."

***

The following weekend, Charlie and Katherine found themselves running from the T commuter train to the Amtrak Northeast Regional at the Back Bay Station. Katherine flopped breathlessly into her seat as Charlie hoisted their suitcase into the overhead rack.

"After two weeks of moving all that luggage, this feels so easy," he said. He put an arm behind her neck and nuzzled her gently.

"For once, I'm happy to let you do it. Next month, we'll let *Chichigo* here carry it." She patted her belly.

"I had no idea that your family were so Native. The language is beautiful. I thought the Pawtucket were extinct."

"It has been easier and safer to let the white men think that, than to be re-organized out of a real existence." She raised an eyebrow. "Look at what happened to the others."

"I know about the Seminole, Cherokee, Mohawk, Sioux—what a nightmare." He gazed at the Long Island sound out the window. "Your grandmother is some kind of leader, that's obvious. Nigå, right?"

"Actually, any elder is called a nigå. Gramma is the saunksqua, which is a female sågamå."

"Sagamore?"

"Yes, occasionally one of the men is elected sågamå. Our structure would never survive the colonial, then the

American, way of looking at things. Our identity flows from the mother, and it was a group of women survivors of the 1633 epidemic who adapted our culture. Because women were ignored until recent times, it was relatively easy to stay out of sight. So, the *Ninnuok*, the People, survived intact, albeit without any official recognition from any government."

"Amazing. I'm also amazed that you speak Pawtucket, too. I never knew."

"Nothing like Mom and Gramma, but I try."

"So, is this one going to be half-Indian?" He passed his hand gently over her bulge, which kicked out suddenly.

"Nope. Full-blooded Pawtucket. Like I said, the identity flows from the mother—completely."

"Wow. That's cool."

***

Three weeks later, Katherine dreamed of drowning in Shad Creek, with fish slithering between her legs. The pressure on her womb felt suddenly less. She snapped awake, aware of the wetness under her.

"Charlie! My water broke."

He rolled from the bed and stood in a single, smooth movement, then bent down to help her up.

"It's been hot sleeping on that plastic cover, but I'm glad we got it now." While she slid off the bloody, wet sheet, he took her nightgown from the back of the bedroom door and helped her into it. "Are you good to take the car?"

"Of course, it's not that far—ooh!" She bent over and took a deep breath to let the pain pass. "But let's get going." He helped her to the bathroom.

Less than a half-hour later, they walked into the emergency room at George Washington University hospital. Her contractions were already three minutes apart, and as painful as she had ever felt anything, even when her battered body awoke from the coma after her crash at the Lagunitas Challenge. The nursing staff recognized the couple from Lamaze classes, and quickly ushered them to a room to change and prep…

Emily Marian Hampstead shot into her father's hands, sliding past the nurse midwife who was guiding the infant out. Katherine gave a tremendous whoosh as the pressure and the pain suddenly vanished, leaving her muscles quivering. Charlie caught the baby like a football, cradling her in his bent arms. Emily let out a cough followed by a deafening wail. Katherine recovered her breath as the attending physician exchanged nods with the midwife. She let Charlie clip the umbilical cord and bring the baby to her mother.

As soon as Emily felt Katherine's body under her, she turned away from his hands and latched onto Katherine's left breast. The new mother wasn't quite ready, but Emily sucked long and hard, until the milk dropped. The infant's efforts quieted into a happy rhythm.

"I have never seen such a determined baby," said the midwife. "Or one with such smooth skin. Usually, they look more wrinkled than that." She stroked the back of the baby. "So taut."

The attending physician, a thirty-something woman with bright blue eyes and black hair, stepped up.

Katherine had asked for Doctor Lara Prescott to be her attending, after meeting most of the OB/GYN staff. Lara typically let the midwives and Lamaze-trained fathers take care of the birth, though she was always nearby during delivery.

"That has to be the shortest labor on record," Lara said as she warmed up her stethoscope on a sterile bandage. "Let's take her vitals." She wrapped the special cuff on Emily's flopping right arm. Her expression darkened as she read the gauge. "Her blood pressure is way high, even for a newborn."

Katherine took the doctor's wrist. "My father warned me about this. Please give it a day or two before trying to treat it. I was the same. Emily's body should expand quickly to accommodate the blood and other fluids."

"Okay, Katherine, but we won't release you two unless it comes down." She turned to examine Katherine's birth canal as the midwife and Charlie dealt with the afterbirth…

Emily's blood pressure was normal when she and Katherine went home after only two nights in the hospital. By then, Louise and Marian were waiting at the little apartment in Foggy Bottom. Katherine complained playfully that with nothing to do but nurse and sleep, she would sign up for a marathon and get out of the house.

***

Katherine woke to the smell of coffee and bacon, and the pressure in her breasts. She felt the cold air from the empty place next to her and turned her head to the crib. As if on cue, an impatient wail came from the layette inside.

Charlie came out of the bathroom, tying the bathrobe around his muscular frame.

"Breakfast, I think." He picked up their daughter and brought her to the bed. Katherine sat up against the headboard and opened the front of her night shift.

"You three are going to spoil me." She said as Emily latched on. Katherine sighed with relief. "And I will so miss them when they go home this weekend."

"Makes me wonder how your dad is doing in the house by himself."

"He's fine. He got used to this sort of routine early, with Mom making three or four field trips every year for research."

"Working in the hospital, he might not have noticed she was gone."

Katherine chuckled. "Maybe not."

When Emily was fed and burped, they dressed, then joined Marian and Louise in the dining area.

"Opening a bank today?" asked Louise, taking in Charlie's conservative suit.

"Interviews and meetings." He poured two mugs of coffee, while Marian set a plate of bacon and eggs in front of Katherine. From her mother's lap, Emily looked around with wide-eyed curiosity. They knew she was taking in everything.

Charlie left after breakfast. Marian played with Emily, while Katherine and Louise cleared the table. Louise cleaned up. Katherine went to the study where she and Charlie had their workstations. She booted up her computer to check her email. An email from Mary Washington University in Fredericksburg caught her eye. She skipped to the middle of the list of incoming messages and opened it.

"Omigod. Mom! Gramma!" The other women came into the study. "Mary Washington University wants to meet. This is from the English Department, not HR."

Louise said, "I'm surprised they haven't sent a limo to pick you up, with the reputation you built in school."

The rest of the summer flew by. Louise and Marian extended their stay to watch Emily, while Katherine went to Fredericksburg. The interview was almost a formality, because the faculty had been following Katherine since she began publishing as an undergraduate. Her work on overlooked female authors was already part of the curriculum at Mary Washington and other schools with Women's Studies majors. Instead of Louise and Marian going home, Martin came south.

By the time school started, the Hampsteads had a new daughter, a new house, a new car, new jobs, and a new life looking ahead.

DADDEEE‼

EMILY SQUEALED WITH DELIGHT, as she sprinted across the sidewalk toward the man riding up to the curb cut by the entrance to Colonial Elementary School.

Charlie Hampstead swung his long leg over his saddle, leaned his bike against the wall, and crouched down to catch the handlebars of Emily's bike flying into him. Emily always pedaled as fast as she could to drive into her father's arms.

"Ooof! You're getting too strong, Emily." Straddling her front wheel, he squeezed the bubbly six-year-old in a bear hug. "Race me home?"

"Not on the sidewalk, she won't." Katherine said from her position on the edge of the road. She smiled at her husband and daughter. "Maybe the last stretch to the house." There was a bike path through the park that led past the back yard of their house.

"Okay, Mommy. Come on, Daddy!" Emily started down the sidewalk.

"Emily!" Katherine shouted. "You're too fast. Stop. Now!" She motioned to the little girl. "If you can ride like that, it's time to join us out here. But stay between Daddy and me, and follow the rules, like we practiced."

The trio made its way down the bike lane to the edge of the park. They crossed the sidewalk to the bike path that led straight across the fields. Emily raced ahead, ringing her bicycle bell to warn pedestrians and dogs. The walkers knew her and waved a friendly hello as she zipped past. Charlie and Katherine greeted their neighbors as they chased the little speed demon.

"Charlie, she's clocking 10 kilometers per hour!"

"Amazing, huh?"

"On that heavy little one-speed?"

"Clearly, she's her mother's daughter," he said as they pulled up to the back gate. "Think what she could do with gears." Emily had already opened the gate and walked her bike into the yard. "Do you think she might be big enough for a 20-inch bike?" he asked. They locked the gate and walked their bikes to the garage.

"No. Not yet, but with this growth spurt she might be big enough by her birthday."

As on most Friday afternoons, the van outside the garage was fueled and packed. A pair of BMC Time Machine bikes graced the roof like a fantasy crown. The family quickly stored their road bikes, gathered their rolling duffel bags and the food from the refrigerator.

"Daddy, can we take my bike, too?"

Charlie looked at Katherine. She closed the lid on the cooler and shrugged.

"Why not?"

"Yippee!" Emily ran to the side of the garage and wheeled her bike to the back of the van. She handed it up to her father, who arched his eyebrows in surprise as he took it.

"Soon, we'll have you hanging the bike yourself, young lady."

Emily giggled. She opened the rear door and climbed into the booster seat. She had her seat belt pulled out and clicked before Katherine got to the door. With a smile, her mother closed the door and got into the passenger seat. Charlie made a final check of the van, the attachments for the bikes, and the garage. Then he climbed into the van while Katherine clicked the remote control to lower the garage door.

"How far this time, Daddy?"

"Not far. Sandbridge is only 170 miles away — maybe three hours or so."

"Okay." Emily reached down to her stuffed Tigger on the seat and pulled the worn toy into her lap. Soon, her parents were smiling and trying not to laugh at the happy sounds of another Tigger adventure coming from the back seat. This time, Tigger was racing an unnamed bear on a single-track trail in the George Washington National Forest. The stuffed tiger almost lost when the bear fell on him, but quickly bounded up (as Tiggers are wont to do) and leaped a few logs that the heavier animal could not clear. Dashing to the bottom of the hillside, Tigger easily won by several lengths. All the animals in the Hundred-Acre Wood came out to celebrate. In his exuberance, Tigger smacked the back of Katharine's head.

"Ouch!"

"Sorry, Mommy. Tigger got carried away."

Charlie signaled a right turn and took the ramp to the rest area. "About time for a break. Bathroom, anyone?" While Katherine and Emily went to the ladies' room, he stretched outside the van, passed by the men's room, then joined them in the food court.

Properly fortified, they resumed their trip. Katharine drove the second half. Charlie played charades with

Emily, looking around his headrest and making faces at his delighted daughter.

One of Katherine's colleagues at Mary Washington University had lent them her condo on the beach. She was happy to have Katherine use it in the off-season and save her a trip to check on it. They settled into the house, then drove to the supermarket for last-minute fresh items that they had not brought.

Katherine's phone rang between the roast salmon and au gratin potatoes, and the fruit and cheese. Their friend Scotty Rehnquist confirmed that he and Sarah would be there at six in the morning to take charge of Emily and her bike.

The next morning, the Rehnquists followed the Hampsteads on their bicycles to the Little Island parking lot, the gathering place for the race. It was a familiar routine. The two couples had been best man and maid-of-honor for their respective weddings. About the time Emily came along, Scotty and Sarah had eased out of the triathlon circuit and volunteered to tend Emily so that Katherine and Charlie could continue to compete.

Emily parked her bike by the Rehnquist van and helped set the table under the tailgate tent that served as support headquarters for the Hampsteads and their fans. Scotty held Emily up, so she could see her parents swimming across Shipps Bay.

"You're getting heavy, Em," he said as he let her down when Katherine appeared on the shore and ran to the transition area. "Next year, you'll be holding me up!" Emily giggled and swatted his knee.

Charlie was right behind his wife. Emily ran to the railing to watch them disappear. A few moments later, they appeared on the mount line. They were almost out of sight by the time the next contestants took off. A smooth transition often made the difference in a triathlon, and the Hampsteads could change faster than anyone.

Emily rode her bike to the mount line at the entrance to the Back Bay National Wildlife refuge. She knew that the contestants would be coming there for the run. Sarah rode with her. Scotty stayed near the transition area, in case he was needed. Katherine showed up, chased by Charlie. Scotty ran beside the road, cheering them on. Emily jumped up and down and shouted as her parents waved passing her. They were out of sight on the path for about ten minutes. Charlie had caught up, but in the last 15 meters, Katherine burst ahead to win the event. The other contestants flowed over the finish line in a great flood.

Katherine and Charlie took a moment to pick up their daughter and give her a big hug. She loved the smell of these moments and their sweat on the front of her body. They put her down and stretched until it was time for the podium ceremony.

Over drinks in the seaside condo, the Rehnquists and Hampsteads celebrated and plotted the rest of the season.

"I'm glad we left the competitive circuit when we did, " said Sarah to Katherine. "I'd hate to be watching your butt all season."

"I wouldn't mind that," quipped Scotty, "but we've having great fun with Emily here." He wiggled his eyebrows, which made the little girl giggle.

"How long do you think you can keep this up?" asked Sarah.

"I don't know," said Katherine, "but we're thinking seriously of focusing on cycling. Maybe gravel or MTB."

"This might be our last tri season," said Charlie.

"I'm amazed by your swimming, Kath," said Sarah. "Isn't that your fastest event?"

"Yes, but I've always considered myself a cyclist first. I'm from Marin County, remember."

Scotty rose to get the wine and refill their glasses. "Why don't you let us take you to dinner? You always treat us to dinner here whenever we do this."

"It's our thank-you," said Charlie. "I know you'd come help us anyway, but we really appreciate your staying with Emily."

"Besides, this way we get to control what we eat after the race."

"And Charlie makes a mean chicken piccata. You can't get that eating out."

"I agree." Scotty set the wine bottle back on the sideboard. "Here's to another great season."

They toasted, Emily with ginger ale, the grownups with a 2005 Riesling.

Scotty and Sarah left after dinner. Emily carried things to the kitchen while her parents did the dishes. After her bath and changing into pajamas, she sat in Charlie's lap and read a story to Tigger.

"Heffalump," said Charlie, when she stopped with her finger on a long word.

"Heffalump…" Emily yawned when she finished the story. She felt a happy drowsiness as her father heaved her over his shoulder and walked gently to the bedroom. Her mother caught Tigger as the toy slipped from the girl's hands. She breathed in the smell of their faces as they kissed her good night. She was waking up in the Hundred Acre Wood before they had the light turned off.

***

Emily stepped into the sunshine at the front door of her school. Her new, 20-inch bike was still the smallest one locked to the rack outside. Few parents let their children ride to school, and she was the only second-grader who rode. Her parents always accompanied her, and she loved their little commuting parade each day, especially now that they let her ride in the bike lane with them instead of the sidewalk.

She unlocked her bike and stood by the stairs, looking for her father or mother. The driveway was full of SUVs and vans, most of them idling with that distinctive stench of cold engines. She straddled her bike and got ready to ride as her father and mother appeared in the street beyond the student pick-up area. She squirmed to blast toward them, but they had been quite stern about her not leaving the entrance until they got there.

Emily heard a popping sound coming from the main door, then a fire alarm on the outside of the building. *Surely, they don't want me to go into a fire,* she thought. She eased her bike out to the sidewalk and waited for her parents in the grass just outside the wall between the school building and the driveway.

She heard screaming from the building, followed by more popping sounds. Some parents left their cars and ran toward the entrance. Sirens wailed from the main highway.

Scared now, Emily got off her bike and crouched up against the wall. Her mother and father both leaped the curb from the street and began pedaling towards her.

"Mommy!"

Katherine was in the lead. She swung off her bicycle, dropping it in the grass. She wrapped her arms around Emily and pulled her close. More popping noises from the school.

Katherine and Emily turned and looked at Charlie Hampstead as he swung off his bicycle, coasting toward them. He jerked sharply and fell to the left. His bicycle coasted forward and crashed on the sidewalk. He lay still. Very still.

"Charlie!" Katherine stood and began to move toward her husband. At that moment, police officers in combat gear converged on the entrance. Two of them grabbed her while a third picked up the stunned Emily and led them away from the entrance to the school.

"Daddeee!"

Her father did not move. As the officer carried her around the corner, she saw an ambulance pull up. Then more popping noises and staccato bursts. Then quiet. The radios on the policemen mumbled something she could not understand.

The officer holding her gave her to her mother. Two of them went back around the corner. The third stayed with them.

Katherine crushed Emily in her arms and began to shake. Emily knew that her father would not get up. She sobbed into her mother's chest, even as Katherine's tears wet her hair.

MAKEUP

"MOM, DON'T YOU USE MAKEUP?" Emily asked as Katherine came downstairs to the kitchen. The girl was pouring coffee into a mug. She handed it to her mother.

Katherine took the mug and held it, not moving from the end of the table. *What is this about?* she thought.

"Well, yes – a little. Sometimes. You've seen me put it on in the bathroom. Why?"

"Because some of the girls at school are wearing it. It's so obvious, and it stinks."

"Stinks? Do you mean maybe too much?"

"Well, yeah. At recess a group of us were sniffing different lipsticks and testing perfumes on our wrists. They were so excited, but I couldn't wait to wash it off in the restroom before class."

Katherine noticed what her daughter had not said: she was trying hard to fit in with the kids at her new school.

Emily sniffed the pot before putting it back on its base. "This coffee smells better than those perfume testers."

Katherine went to the counter. She took some bread from the bread box and popped it into the toaster. "Eggs?"

"Sure." Emily took a package of bacon and the eggs from the refrigerator. While Katherine put the bacon on to cook, her daughter whipped some scrambled eggs with spices and set it by the range for her mother to cook in the bacon grease.

"Where do you keep your makeup? Joanna's mom has one of those long tables with a fancy mirror and tons of bottles and jars on it."

"In the top drawer of my dresser. Do you want to see?"

"Maybe later. What do you have?"

Katherine set the bacon on some paper towels, then poured the scrambled eggs into the skillet. Emily moved the butter dish from the counter to the table.

"Let me think. I have a lipstick, and a small bottle of perfume that your father gave me shortly after we were married. A tube of mascara, and– and– I guess that's it."

"No creams or foundation?"

Katherine laughed gently. "No. Not yet, anyway. I do use a moisturizer with Vitamin E in it, and sunblock, of course."

"That's not really makeup."

"No, I guess not."

"I've never smelled anything on you."

"The idea is not to smell or see the cosmetic, but to look as if it's natural. If you don't need the help, you don't need the makeup."

Katherine moved the food to the dishes that Emily brought from the cabinet.

"Have you ever compared your eyelashes to others?"

"Not really," said Emily. "What do you mean?"

"Why do you think women wear mascara?"

"To make their eyes pop. That's what the girls at recess said."

"What if you already had long, thick lashes?"

"You wouldn't need mascara?"

"Exactly. You and I have the kind of lashes that don't usually need mascara."

"So, why wear it at all?"

"I can't speak of other women, but sometimes, I'll wear it at a nighttime event, like a dance or going to a dark nightclub, because my features would not be as visible in low light. I might also wear it when giving a presentation before a large audience. The same reason actors wear makeup up on a stage."

"What did Daddy think?"

Katherine smiled.

"Like most men, he was clueless about it. On a date, he asked me why I never wore mascara or lipstick when I had put them on specifically for him that night." They snorted. "See what I mean about not seeing or smelling the makeup?"

"I get it." Emily speared a piece of bacon and spread some scrambled eggs on it. "What about lipstick?"

"Again, have you compared yourself to anyone else?" Emily shook her head. "You and I have full lips. Some women have pale lips, or thin lips, and they want to bring out their lips better. I use a sun-blocking lip balm with some natural color in it. That's enough for me."

"Some of the girls have lipsticks to go with what they're wearing."

"If you are already using lipstick regularly, I can understand that. Some women change colors to suit their mood or to try something new. I just never felt the need."

"Isn't makeup supposed to make you sexy?"

Katherine laughed.

"That's what the manufacturers would have you believe. But if it were true, would they need to advertise so much?"

"It doesn't work?"

"Well, it can help if done right, but often it backfires, because it sends the wrong signal to the intended target, male or female."

"Huh?"

"What do *you* think sexy looks like?"

"I don't know. I don't get half of what the other girls say. I think they're making up stuff to feel cool. I've read about it, but boys don't make me feel anything at all. I mean, some of them are friendly, but I can tell that's not what the girls are talking about."

"Part of puberty, dear. You'll get the feelings soon enough."

"With my period?"

"Maybe before." Katherine sipped her coffee. "Anyway, in my humble opinion, sexy has nothing to do with makeup. We respond to the body shape of the sex that attracts us. Makeup can't do a thing for your fitness, your height, the curve of your hips, or your poise. Trust me, a woman walking erect with athletic grace, maybe with some rhythm to her gait, will catch their attention faster than the most expensive perfume or lipstick."

"Really?"

"It's an animal thing, wired into us."

"Would I be considered sexy?" Almost immediately, Emily caught her breath, embarrassment etched on her face.

"Oh, my darling daughter, yes! You are the sexiest twelve-year-old on the planet." She reached out and gently pinched Emily's cheek. "The confidence you exude, the way you walk and talk – they surprise everyone. The boys at Chisholm Middle School aren't ready for it yet, but I have seen the looks on the older boys and men when you walk by them."

"But I don't have boobs, like the other girls."

"The ones in your class?" Emily nodded. "Half of them are probably wearing stuffed training bras. Don't worry about it. You'll never look like Dolly Parton, but you'll have what you need when you need it."

They cleared the table and put the dishes in the dishwasher. Emily washed the skillet, while Katherine poured the rest of the coffee into her commuter travel mug.

***

Dean Shanholtz stopped as Katherine walked past her in the hall outside the dean's office.

"Good morning, Katherine. You look pensive today."

Katherine snapped her attention to her boss.

"Sorry, Margaret. Yes. One of those milestones in parenting. Emily was asking about makeup at breakfast today. It's all the rage among the seventh-grade girls at recess, it seems."

"Ah, yes. At least Emily asked. My two were brought home by our local deputy. They were walking down Main Street looking like hookers." They shared a chuckle. "Not one of my better moments as a parent. Looking back, I'm glad we were living in such a small town."

"It's great that you can laugh now," said Katherine. "I think Emily was calmer than I was, though I tried to hide it." She sighed. "If this is seventh grade, I hate to think what lies ahead."

"Katherine, don't worry about Emily. She's the most level-headed young woman I've ever met, except maybe for her mother, of course."

The dean started to turn, then stopped.

"What did you tell her, if I may ask? All these years later, I have always wondered what I might have done differently."

Katherine stopped to think. "I guess I just answered her questions. She did not seem impressed by what she learned on the playground but accepted my opinion."

"Which was?"

"That she wouldn't need it much, if ever."

"Well, she does take after you. I'm sure you'll teach her well. Your mascara and lipstick are so discrete that I sometimes wonder if you wear any at all."

Katherine wasn't, but she clamped down on a response.

"See you at the colloquium, Katherine. Have a good day." The dean turned to her office.

MARK

KATHERINE HAMPSTEAD STOPPED at the double doors to the banquet hall. Charlie had always paused before entering a room, and she had picked up the habit. She looked to the side, half-expecting him to take her hand.

But he was not there.

A crushing sadness almost made her turn around and run home. It had been years since she had stood outside Colonial Elementary in Fredericksburg, holding their daughter, watching Charlie die in a burst of gunfire from inside the school. Years of holding Emily in her arms at night, as they shed tears after their shared nightmares. Years of fleeing to the ladies' room when yet another well-meaning colleague or friend asked how she was doing. Years of struggling to concentrate on her classes and her research as the image of the handsome, intelligent, funny, and hopelessly romantic Marine officer kept appearing just out of reach.

The annual fall convocation reception was an occasion to introduce new faculty from all the schools, to meet friends and colleagues after the summer absences, and hopefully to make new friends outside one's own department. As one of the honorees of the event, she could hardly turn down the invitation.

…Two years ago, Dean Shanholtz of Wichita State University had finally convinced her to teach in the Women's Studies Department. Katherine needed to escape Virginia and the memories. Feminist literature scholars were few on the ground, and Wichita State had been trying to recruit her for three years. They brought her aboard with full tenure and offered her two teaching assistants for the undergraduate courses. They could not match her salary as a tenured professor at Mary Washington University, but the chance to work in the second oldest women's studies department in the country and her need to escape made her waffle—until one night in Fredericksburg.

She and Emily sat reading in the living room. Katherine looked at her daughter, intently focused on her copy of *The Wizard of Oz*. The floor lamp behind the chair caught Emily's auburn hair like a halo. Katherine's heart swelled as she watched the girl enjoying the same books she had enjoyed at that age, losing herself in wonderful worlds, escaping the tragedy that clouded this one.

As if sensing her mother's eyes, Emily raised her head.

"Isn't Kansas where that school wants you to teach?"

"Yes, dear. Wichita State University."

"Do they really have tornadoes there?"

"Yes. That's why almost all the houses have sturdy basements."

"It's really flat, too, isn't it?" Her mother nodded. "I could ride super-fast there."

Katherine smiled. "That, too. I think the ramps on the interstate are the steepest hills around Wichita." Emily was already a speed demon among the gentle hills on either side of the Rappahannock River, giving Katherine some pleasant exercise when they rode together.

"Why don't we move there?" Emily closed her book. She kept a finger in her place, a gesture that reminded Katherine of the girl's father. "I could have adventures like Dorothy." She made a silly grin and raised her eyebrows inquiringly.

"Darling, Dorothy —"

"I know, Mommy. She's not real. But I've never been to Kansas or seen a tornado. Could we come back if we don't like it?"

Katherine caught herself and thought about it. She knew that she could apply to almost any university in the country and find work. That Dean Shanholtz in Wichita had been so persistent was partly why she was even considering their offer. She sighed.

"We could – or go somewhere else, too. Do you want to move?"

"I think so. I mean, I know you're not happy here."

Katherine could hear the innocence in the comment but still felt a blow.

"Why do you say that?"

"Mommy, I may only be ten years old, but anyone can see how you carry Daddy around. I miss him, too, and everything around here keeps reminding me of him. I've never lived anywhere else, so I don't know what moving would be like."

Katherine thought, *Out of the mouths of babes…* She smiled and put out her arms. Emily slipped the bookmark from the end table to her book and ran to her mother. They snuggled in silence for a while.

"Let's do it," said Katherine. "I'll start working on it tomorrow."

Once she made her choice, it had taken the rest of the semester and the whole next year to see her doctoral students to their degrees, help Mary Washington recruit the most promising one to replace her, then formally apply to Kansas State. Having a goal helped with the nightmares and the depression. It seemed to help Emily, too. They still had nightmares and flashbacks, but they were learning to deal with the triggers, and the nightmares occurred less and less often…

Now, Katherine scanned the crowded room, her ears aching from a hundred voices bouncing off the walls. She gritted her teeth and waited for the panic to wash over her. She had expected it, but the intensity of the feeling always terrified her.

She took a deep breath and stepped into the crowd, looking for a familiar face. Dean Margaret Shanholtz was holding court in a corner to the right. Katherine knew only half of them, but the dean spotted her and waved her over.

"Katherine, come meet some new people." Margaret took her arms and turned her to the group. "You already know Lisette and Yvonne in your department, but I have corralled three gentlemen who have never met a feminist before.

"Jim Abernathy just joined the History Department; Jerry Kwang is in Mathematics; and Mark Dempsey here is in Aeronautical Engineering. Gentlemen, this is Katherine Hampstead, who comes to us from Mary Washington." Handshakes all around. The historian's hand was limp, and the mathematician bowed as he shook her hand.

Katherine turned to the engineer. His firm handshake came with a smile that included his eyes. The tailored sport coat fit his broad shoulders and slim figure more fashionably than any professor that Katherine had ever seen. Gray eyes, which did not drop to her chest, but looked directly into hers. Sandy hair cut short, but not as short as a Marine.

They held hands rather longer than usual, but Katherine did not feel her usual reaction. At last, she took a breath, and they broke the handshake.

"Engineering?" Katherine glanced at the dean. "Margaret, you were right. I spend so much time in our building that I forgot we teach things like that."

Mark chuckled and lifted a champagne flute from a passing server. He handed it to Katherine. "If you like, I could give you a tour. We have all sorts of cool toys in our research labs."

"I think I would like that. Thank you." *Now, why did I say that?* Katherine tried to cover her discomfiture with a broad smile. She engaged the other two men in conversation, then let Margaret introduce her to some old hands in the College of Liberal Arts and the Central Administration.

***

The next morning, Katherine had no afternoon classes, so she was packing up to go home when the phone rang. She recognized Mark's voice: deep and confident, with a slightly Southern accent.

"The dean dragged you off too quickly last night. May we continue the conversation over lunch?"

"Today?"

"If you're free, yes. I'm on campus this morning, but I just taught my last class for the day."

"Me, too. Sure. I haven't had a chance to check out options here. How about you?"

"There's a Thai place on the way back to my office."

"Thai is fine. Let's do it."

A half-hour later, they were sitting in a booth. Katherine was trying to make sense of her conflicted emotions. Mark made her feel at ease, both with his careful driving, and with the way he listened without interrupting. He seemed sincerely interested in her, and asked questions rather than volunteering opinions. Nevertheless, she was keenly aware that she had not been out with anyone except Emily since Frank Armistead got orders to Korea and left Fredericksburg last year.

After the server left with their orders, they looked at each other silently. She finally broke the silence.

"Where is your office? This is hardly on the way to the Aerospace Engineering Department."

"I'm an adjunct. I teach an undergraduate course every other day. My regular job is at McConnell Air Force Base."

"Is that why you look like a military officer?"

"Maybe. I am an Army brat and a retired Air Force officer."

"Tell me about your work here."

"It's a small company that specializes in research projects for the Air Force. It's cheaper and quicker to hire us to dig into a problem and research it than to detail active-duty personnel through the training needed, then put them on the problem."

"Really? I thought defense contractors cost more than the military personnel they replace."

"Not in our little niche. We can recruit the special skills already trained and focus fully on the problem without trying to operate an airwing, repair aircraft or manage an air base."

"Lots of short-term projects?"

"Yes, but something new always comes up before we deliver the ones we're working on." The server returned with their red and green curries, then replenished their water.

She looked past his shoulder and stared at the sky after the server left. She had not felt this relaxed with anyone since—

"Katherine?" She snapped her attention back to his concerned face. The tightness in her chest subsided.

"I'm sorry. I zoned out there."

He looked at her intently. "More than zone. And I think I understand. I Googled you after the reception, so I know what happened to you and Emily. That's your daughter's name, isn't it?"

"Yes."

"That's why I haven't asked you why you left Mary Washington or anything else about it." He sipped his water. "Instead, tell me what Margaret Atwood is like. I read your interview. She must be fascinating."

"She is, and a real piece of work…" For the rest of the meal, Mark quizzed her about her research on feminist authors and her book about nineteenth-century women who were writing ahead of their time. She felt the same thrill she got explaining her work to eager young students, but for the sheer pleasure of it: no baggage of grades or tests or evaluations.

It was three o'clock when she happened to look at her wrist.

"Omigod. Emily gets home at four. I have to go."

Mark signaled for the bill. She took out her wallet.

"I asked for this. Let's argue about paying next time, please."

"Well, okay." She scowled enough to let him know that she did not care for empty gallantry. He grinned.

As they approached her parking place on campus, he said, "I still want to give you that tour, and let you fight me about paying for dinner. Could we do this again, maybe on Friday night?"

"Let me check my schedule and see what Emily is doing. I'll call you tomorrow."

She let herself out of the car before he could open the door to go around the car. She waved as she got into hers and drove quickly away.

***

Friday night, Mark picked her up at their new house in Newton, twenty-six miles north of the university. Emily had been invited to a sleep over at the church with the girls in the youth group. With the extra time, they had agreed to dinner and a movie.

Over dinner, they finally got around to the personal stuff of getting to know each other. Mark had been an aviation engineering duty officer, not a pilot. Katherine was surprised that he had never married.

"I had a couple of chances, but the Air Force kept cutting my tours short and sending me halfway across the world. Hard to sustain a relationship like that."

"Why would they do that?"

"I gathered something of a reputation as a change agent and troubleshooter. The word got around, and I found myself drafted by a friend of the last general I worked for, and so on."

"When did you retire?"

"Three years ago. I was in Virginia first, which was great, because my parents live in Lancaster County. But last spring, I was sent to McConnell, so here I am."

"Until a new problem crops up in Korea or Germany?"

"I don't think so. The company is getting new clients among the aviation industry in Wichita, so I won't be moving away early."

"That's good, I guess."

"I think so, especially now that I've met you." He held up his wine in a salute. Katherine wondered why that did not sound like a pick-up line when he said it.

Later, neither could remember what the movie was. They had another date the following week, then, a month after the convocation reception, she invited him home for dinner to meet Emily. That afternoon, he attended a colloquium at the College, at which she was presenting some of her research. Over dinner, he confided that the discussion made him uncomfortable.

"It sounded like they hated your ideas. So much criticism." He said as he passed the roast potatoes. "How did you stay so calm?"

"The whole point is to murder-board the ideas." She started the fish around. "I don't think they hated it. In fact, I was pleased that they were so engaged. The two loudest critics – Smith and Morley – told me afterwards how much they liked it."

"Mom came home from one in Fredericksburg where they were all quiet and polite," said Emily. "She was miserable for a week."

"Takes the concept of constructive criticism to a new level, I think." He smiled and shook his head.

***

The following week, they had another date. Katherine's stress level between dates rose, as she found herself churning between guilt, pleasure, fear, and anticipation. *This is stupid,* she told herself a dozen times, but the conflicting feelings kept chasing each other as she worked her way through the week.

What made it worse was that Mark had suggested the Officers' Club at the air base, where there was dancing as well as dinner. She had not danced since Charlie's death. She was as thrilled at the prospect of close contact with Mark as she was terrified. Three times during the week, she picked up the phone to call off the date on some pretext but put it back before dialing.

This time, Mark walked around the car and held the passenger door for her. Katherine scowled, but he smiled. Emily waved from the stoop.

"Don't hurry back, y'all." She smiled and waved. Katherine scowled at her, too.

"What was that all about?" he asked as he buckled in.

"She talked me into not hiring a babysitter, and I'm a nervous wreck. She's been rubbing it in ever since."

"She *is* old enough to babysit, you know."

"That's what she said." Katherine let out an exasperated sigh.

"And she's sharp and responsible."

"This isn't about Emily. I'm the one with the problem."

He fed onto Interstate 135 and settled into the right lane at the speed limit. That allowed everyone to pass them without annoying someone by being too slow.

"May I ask about the problem?"

"Part of it is the knee-jerk reaction of a mother to her child's growing independence. But she has been getting bullied at school since we arrived, and I only just found out."

Mark let the silence hang for a while.

"And?"

"And I taught her a few self-defense moves that my grandmother taught me. Now I'm afraid of what might happen."

"Is the bullying on record?"

"It is now. She reported it this week, and I lodged a complaint with the principal."

"Are you worried about her being hurt?"

"Of course. And about her getting in trouble if there is a fight."

He pulled left to pass a rusty pickup truck towing a flat trailer just barely above the minimum speed limit. When he pulled back in, he drove in silence for a while.

"If anything happens, call me. I want to help, and the law firm we retain covers all the different specialties."

"But—"

"No buts, Katherine. Please. Let me help. I care about Emily; I would want to help her for her own sake, not just yours." He glanced quickly at her. "Does that make any sense?"

"I guess so. You know I hate being catered to—"

"If you are going to say I'm doing the knight in shining armor routine, don't. We have single fathers in our company, and I treat them the same as the single mothers."

Katherine leaned back in her seat and thought about what was different about Mark. When he acted like a gentleman, it did not feel condescending; it felt right. By now, she knew that he was color-blind on race and deeply empathetic. She sighed and smiled.

"Thanks. I'll call if anything happens." They rode in silence.

The traffic flowed off I-135 to Southeast Boulevard, the connector to I-35 and the exit for the air base. Fifteen minutes later, he parked in front of the club.

Dinner was served at tables around the dance floor. Considering the mix of active duty and retired personnel there, at least three generations mingled on the floor and seemed to enjoy every genre of music from Big Band to hip-hop.

Katherine was slicing a piece of her grilled wild-caught salmon when she happened to look past Mark's shoulder. She saw a Marine in service greens coming in the door. The fish on her fork paused in mid-air as the aviator wings shimmered and dissolved, and the face morphed into—

Mark grabbed her wrists as the food tumbled to her plate. "Katherine! Look at me!" His voice was gentle, but insistent. Katherine held her breath as the scream in her chest struggled with Mark's call through her panic. After a few seconds, she let out the air slowly.

"Thank you. I'm sorry. I—"

"Don't apologize." Mark looked behind him. "That's Captain McDonough. He's stationed with the Twenty-Second Air Refueling Wing on some sort of exchange program. He probably has the duty tonight to be in uniform."

"I thought I saw Charlie." Katherine pulled her hands back gently and gathered herself.

"I know. It was written all over your face."

They finished the main course without talking. Katherine continued to seek a calm place. After a while, she realized that Mark did not force her into conversation or try to fill the silence. She felt even more grateful for that than for the sudden reaction to her flashback.

When the server had cleared their plates, Mark asked her to dance. It was a slow number, and she held on to him rather more tightly than she might have. But she felt a need to share physical contact. After two numbers, the band paused, then hit the opening chord of *Start Me Up* by the Rolling Stones. Mark raised his eyebrows, and she nodded. They danced the rest of the set before returning to the table to order dessert.

The band played until midnight.

"I'm not ready to go home," Katherine said. "This has been wonderful. What about you?"

"I don't want the evening to end, either, and tomorrow is Saturday. Want to go clubbing, such as it is in Wichita?"

"No." Katherine rose and put out her hand. "You've seen my house. Show me yours."

"My bachelor pad?" Mark asked with genuine surprise.

"I have a hunch about it."

"Well. It's just a studio apartment in College Hill, but I'd be delighted. Come."

Katherine's hunch was right. The spotless condition of the upscale apartment showed his upbringing in an Army family with high expectations. She turned to him as he closed the door. They shared an embrace. The first kiss was a closed-mouth thing as she struggled to let herself go. Then she relaxed....

Bus Bullies

EMILY STARED at the board covered with dates while Ms. Mumford droned. The dates blurred and faded, as Emily pictured the scene at dinner the night before. Her mother had brought Mr. Dempsey ("call me Mark") home, and Emily was conflicted about it.

On one hand, Mark seemed nice enough. He showed a gentle strength under his quiet manner. He did not interrupt Emily or Katherine, which was saying a lot in Emily's estimation. At twelve years old, she already understood her mother's annoyance at being disrespected in conversation. It bothered Emily, too. That he was fit and handsome in a plain way also counted in his favor. Katherine Hampstead was a champion athlete, though she had left the professional marathon and triathlon circuit when Emily came along. And Emily could see that her mother was comfortable with Mark.

No, more than comfortable. She had not seen that look on her mother's face since the day before her father had died in front of Colonial Elementary School five years ago. It made Emily feel happy and scared at the same time.

Happy to see her mother relaxing in a way she had not seen for more than half of all the time that Emily could remember.

Feeling scared puzzled her. She was not afraid of Mark, so why did she feel that something threatened her and her life with Katherine? Was she afraid that Mark would die, too? Her heart sank at the thought that she and her mother might carry a curse.

"Miss Hampstead?" The blackboard came into focus, as did Ms. Mumford's tight mouth and arched eyebrow. "Daydreaming again?"

"Sorry, ma'am." Emily heard tittering from the rows behind her.

"See me after class."

"Yes, ma'am." Emily blushed fiercely from a combination of embarrassment and dreaded anticipation. Recess would feature more snide remarks and bullying from her classmates.

Emily had only transferred to Chisholm Middle School this year, and quickly found herself out of favor with the cliques of girls who had grown up in Newton. Only three classmates, whose parents were stationed at the big Air Force base in Wichita, did not give her a hard time: two boys and one girl. Still, they would not be caught defending the new girl now that they were being tolerated by the others.

It did not help that she was one of the smallest girls in seventh grade. That most of the riders on her bus were eighth graders made things worse. She had a bruise where Billy Medford had pinched her yesterday. She had slapped him, but he grabbed her wrist and twisted it until it hurt. The rest of the bus laughed until the driver stopped the bus and chewed them out. Still, the smirks and giggles went on until they reached the school.

After class, Emily approached the teacher's desk. She stood there while the class filed out. Only when they were alone did Ms. Mumford speak.

"You weren't daydreaming, were you, Emily?"

"No, ma'am."

"You seem worried about something. Can you tell me?" Emily stood quietly, wringing her fingers. "Are you being bullied?" Emily nodded. "Who?" Emily looked down and closed her lips tightly. "They're not your friends. You don't owe them any loyalty. Who is bullying you?"

Emily looked up at Ms. Mumford. "Everybody and nobody in particular."

"It's more than the bullying, isn't it?" Emily nodded. "Do you think you could talk to someone about it?"

"I don't know anyone that well."

"We're here to help, Emily, not just push dates at you. Nurse Gibson told me that she likes you. Maybe you could talk to her. She won't tell anyone, because that's how nurses and doctors are. Would you go see her?"

"Can I go during recess?" The play period after lunch.

"You don't want to go to recess?"

"No."

Ms. Mumford thought for a moment. "I understand, and I think that seeing the nurse instead of recess is a good idea. Here's a referral slip." She checked some boxes on the top page of the pad on her desk and gave the form to Emily. "You are a bright girl, and you seemed to enjoy this class at first. I would like to see you enjoy it again."

Emily thanked the teacher, shouldered her backpack, and went down the hall. She heard the shouts and laughter of her classmates through the open windows to the schoolyard. Some of the deeper laughter drowned out squeals of pain. She was glad not to be out there.

At the little office that served as an infirmary, Emily found a note on the door:

For emergencies, go to the school office. The nurse will return tomorrow.

Emily dismissed the idea of going to recess immediately. *This is not an emergency, so I don't have to go to the office.*

Instead, she walked to the back of the building, where she knew the maintenance workers had their shops and storerooms. She heard the janitors and the maintenance men talking loudly over their lunches.

Creeping behind the lockers and tables, she found a storeroom that she had discovered when she got lost the first week of school. It held a large quantity of very dusty boxes, which meant that no one ever came in the room. With a door to the outside and to the inside, it made a perfect place to hide. She cleaned off a pair of boxes by the window and took out the Nancy Drew book she had borrowed from her mother.

By using the outside door when the bell rang at the end of recess, she could join the other students in the schoolyard returning to class. Each afternoon, she returned feeling restored and ready to face the afternoon.

In the storage room she escaped into the books she loved. She read novels, and books about explorers, survival, and real-life adventures from around the world. She tracked down books about the women in an article from an issue of *The Guardian* that she found in the library: "Top Ten inspiring female adventurers," by Rosemary Brown. The biographies of Nellie Bly, Gertrude Bell, Bessie Coleman, and others became the stuff of her daydreams.

***

"Miss Hampstead, would you stay a moment?" Ms. Mumford glared at the other students who had stopped. They left quickly. Emily approached the desk.

"First, let me say that I'm pleased that you seem to have recovered your spirits since I sent you to Nurse Gibson. But she told me yesterday that you never went to see her."

Emily bit the inside of her mouth to keep from reacting visibly.

"There was a note on the door that she was out all day."

"Yes, I remember that now. So, why the change?"

"They're not bugging me at recess."

"That's good. Any idea why?"

"No, ma'am."

"Not picking on someone else, are they?"

"I wouldn't know. I haven't seen anything."

"Well, for what it's worth, Nurse Gibson said she'd be happy to meet with you any time about anything. That goes for me, too, Emily."

She pointed at the door, and Emily walked quickly to the next class. She let out her breath at the door, surprised that she had been holding it.

***

"Mom, stop it!"

Katherine put down the phone and leaned her hip on the kitchen counter. Her eyebrows formed a question.

"I'm old enough to be a babysitter myself. Why are you trying to find someone to watch me tomorrow night?"

"But —"

"Go out with Mark. Have a good time. I promise not to burn the house down or to open the door to strangers."

"What will you do?"

"What do you think? Homework. Work on that history paper that's due next week. Maybe I'll stream some pornography on the internet."

"Emily!"

"Just kidding, Mom." She grinned. "C'mon. You worry too much. The only one likely to get in trouble is you, without me there to embarrass you."

Katherine sighed and opened the dishwasher. They put dishes away in companionable silence. Emily collected the trash and hauled the heavy bin to the curb. When she returned, Katherine was sitting in their small living room with a cup of coffee. Emily got herself a glass of orange juice and joined her mother.

"You're starting your growth spurt, Emily."

"How do you know?" She knew she was still shorter than everyone else.

"You've gotten skinny since we moved here, but you're getting stronger in spite of that. Do you feel any different?"

"Nothing hurts."

"What about your emotions?"

"Only that I would like to break Billy Medford's face."

"Anger. That's new. Who is Billy Medford?"

"Eighth grader on the bus. He pinches me when I go by. Sometimes it leaves a bruise. One time I slapped him, but he grabbed my arm and twisted it."

"Emily! That's assault."

"Slapping him?"

"No. Pinching you. What happened after that?"

"Nothing. The other kids think it's funny. They laughed so hard that the driver stopped and chewed everyone out."

"How long has this been going on?"

"Since the first week. Most of the kids on the bus are his friends or they're afraid of him."

"Why?"

"He was retained in sixth grade, so he's older and bigger than anyone else. And he's built like a football player."

"You need to report this to the office."

"And have him and his gang beat me up or something?"

"Is it that bad?"

"That's what happened last year when someone tried to stand up to him at recess. After the fight, Billy and the other kid were suspended for a week, but the other kid never came back. Apparently, he was mugged that night, and his family put him in private school."

"Maybe I should look into private schools too."

"No, Mom. That wouldn't help. I have to live with these creeps later, so I'd rather figure out how to do that now."

They sat in silence while Emily tried to picture ways of getting Billy Medford and the other bullies to leave her alone. For her part, Katherine admired Emily's intention to deal with the challenge. *I couldn't afford private school anyway.*

"Mom, what if I *did* break his face?"

Katherine started to reply then caught herself. She looked long and hard at Emily, then at the pictures of Charlie over the mantle. One in his Marine Corps dress uniform. The other, her favorite, taken as he broke the tape at a marathon race after she was pregnant with Emily. She saw the shape of Charlie's head in Emily's profile.

"I think you should report the bullying to someone first."

"That's whining, isn't it?"

"No." Katherine swung to her daughter, and a dark expression came over her face. "That's a warning. You say he bugs you regularly?"

"Yes."

"When you report it, explain that you intend to defend yourself the next time it happens."

"And?"

"After you report it, I'll add my complaint as an outraged parent. Then, when you break his face – or arm or whatever – your report and my complaint will come out, and they will be at fault for not taking action."

"How do I break his face?"

"Now that's the fun part." Katherine rose and extended her hand. "Come downstairs."

***

The next morning, Emily paused at the front of the bus. She took in the rows of expectant faces, some grinning, some looking worried. Billy Medford pretended to look out the window, his lips in a silent whistle like a cartoon character. The only free seats were in the back of the bus. She took a deep breath and started down the aisle.

As she passed Billy, she felt his fingers on the back of her thigh. She reached down, clamping her right hand on his arm and reaching out to grab his other wrist as he brought it up. That put her face an inch from his.

"Do that again, Medford, and I'll break something!"

The shock on Billy's face gave way to red fury and embarrassment, but by then Emily was already two seats away.

"Sit down, Billy," the driver called. "Let the others get on."

When they arrived at school, Emily went in search of Ms. Mumford before class. The teacher was coming out of the faculty lounge.

"I want to report bullying, Ms. Medford. Where do I go?"

"At last. I have a form in my desk. Come." She led Emily to the social studies classroom.

That afternoon, the Air Force girl told her that Billy was looking for her at recess.

***

Katherine disengaged and looked into Mark's eyes. He smiled and tilted his head to the house.

"No lights on."

"Why do I feel like a teenager creeping in after curfew?" She reached into her purse for her keys.

"Because that's what you look like." He kissed her gently. "I'll call you tomorrow."

He waited at his car while she opened the door, then he drove silently away. Inside, she found a note taped to her bedroom door.

Dear Mom,

Your bathrobe is too long for me, the rolling pin got heavy, and I couldn't find any curlers.

I went to bed.

XXOO.

A smiley face with crossed eyes grinned from the bottom of the page. She smiled and sighed quietly as she took down the note and went to bed herself.

Saturday morning, the smell of coffee snapped Katherine awake. The sun was well up. *I don't remember setting the coffeemaker last night.* She leaped out of bed and went to her closet. Her bathrobe was hung inside out. She grinned and put it on. After a quick peek in the mirror, she followed the aroma.

Emily sat at the kitchen table with the morning newspaper. She got up and went to the coffeemaker.

"Good morning, Doctor Hampstead. I take it you had a satisfactory evening." She handed her mother a mug. "I hope it's okay."

Katherine smelled the rich brew and took a careful taste. "Perfect. Where did you learn to make coffee?"

"Google."

"Of course. I still don't think of that first."

"Well, how was your date?"

"You're pretty cheeky for a twelve-year-old, you know."

"Call me a liberated teenager. Some of my classmates are already dating."

"Omigod, really?"

Emily nodded. "Judging from the litter in the girl's room, there are a lot of periods too."

"Isn't sex education supposed to be in high school?"

"It'll be too late for some of them. I hope they have something new to teach us by then."

Katherine shook her head. "Well, the date was wonderful."

"I guessed that. I watched *Bride of Frankenstein* until two-thirty, then gave up."

"In my bathrobe?" They laughed. Emily sipped her milk and looked steadily at her mother.

"How serious are you and Mark?"

Katherine paused, "I don't know. I only met him at the new faculty orientation party when we arrived. He's an adjunct professor at the Institute for Aviation Research. What? Four dates?"

"And dinner."

"Yes, but long ago, I resolved to bring any man I dated home. They need to know that I come with baggage."

"I'm a suitcase?"

"No, but they have to pass the Emily test."

"I get it. I like Mark. But I also liked the Army colonel in Fredericksburg."

"He was nice, but there was no spark there."

"It's different with Mark, isn't it?"

"I think so—no, I know so."

They sat for a while.

"Mom, if it makes any difference, I don't mind having him hang around all you like."

"Good, because I'd like to have him over again tomorrow. Okay with you?"

"Are you testing the way to a man's heart through his stomach?"

"Maybe."

"It's fine with me."

Katherine stood. "Speaking of food, I need breakfast. What have you planned for today?"

"I had some oatmeal already, but we could fix more. Or we could ride to that waffle place downtown." Emily was wearing a bicycle kit.

"Let's do that. I am so sick of driving all week."

***

Emily shivered at the bus stop Monday morning. It wasn't cold, but she was terrified and excited at the same time. She hoped a stern look would dissuade any moves from Billy, but she also hoped she would be ready if not.

Pausing at the top of the steps, she spotted Billy in his usual seat. The others were staring expectantly, and Emily could feel the frisson of anticipation in the bus.

Billy was looking directly at her this time. She felt her stomach jump before her steady breathing took over.

"Don't, Billy," she called as she started down the aisle.

Sure enough, the pinch came as she passed him.

Emily reached with her left hand and pulled the boy almost out of his seat as she whirled to the left, drawing his left arm across the aisle. She pulled up her right knee into his elbow and heard the pop as it dislocated.

Then she turned back and walked to the open seat in the back of the bus.

An hour later, Emily sat in the sergeant's office at the police department, waiting for her mother to arrive. The driver had called the police. The officers who responded were careful not to ask her any questions.

"We'll let the right people sort this out, but let's get her out of here before the media shows up."

Billy had been taken away by ambulance, screaming. The others got off the bus at school a half-hour late.

Outside, she could hear a commotion.

"What's going on?" she asked the sergeant.

"Reporters and TV crews. Not every day we have this much excitement in Newton."

Emily looked out the window. The reporters were mobbing her mother as she tried to walk to the door. To Emily's surprise, Mark was with her, plowing a path to the door for her.

"Come with me, miss." The sergeant led her to a conference room down the hall. The police chief, Mark, Katherine, the school principal, Doctor Morgan, and a man she did not know were seated around the table. *A lawyer?*

Katherine rose and hugged her daughter. When they sat down, the police chief did the introductions. The stranger was a lawyer, on retainer to Mark's company. *Oh, right,* Emily thought. *Adjuncts are part-timers. He would have another job.*

"This could drag on indefinitely with the media interest," said the police chief. "I wanted to get the principal characters in this affair together without the Medfords. They are threatening to sue the school and Ms. Hampstead—"

"Professor Hampstead or Doctor Hampstead," said Mark. He had cut off both the police chief and Katherine.

Emily had picked up on the policeman's dismissive tone. Mark rolled his hand for the chief to continue.

"Anyway, it appears that young William initiated the exchange that led to his dislocated elbow. And apparently Emily has reported him for repeated assaults over the last six weeks." He looked at the principal, who nodded, keeping her face as impassive as she could manage. "What is your take on this, Ms.—Doctor Hampstead?"

"The school has a problem with bullying on the bus and at recess. If they can get a handle on the problem, I'd rather not see anyone sued. Doctor Morgan and her teachers are my colleagues. I would be willing to work with them on that."

"And the Medfords?"

Katherine exchanged glances with the attorney. "I don't know them personally. If their son stays in the school system, he'll come under whatever measures are put in place to deal with bullies. I heard reports of earlier bullying and even assaults on another student outside school. You may find yourself dealing with William, so you might want to be ready for that. Emily has used the minimum force needed to end a threatening situation, while bringing the attention of the right people to the problem." She looked at the attorney. "Anything to add?"

"Chief, the Medfords could be ruined by taking this to court. They should spend their money on help for William."

The chief looked around the table, then consulted the papers that he had brought with him.

"No one is willing to testify to what happened except Emily and William, so we have nothing to give the prosecutor. The school system will have to deal with

William based on the reports, and my people will watch out for any misbehavior outside of school.

"You are free to go. I'll let you know if we need anything else."

***

"Emily, where were you during recess today?" Emily stopped in the hall. Her mother was *never* home before she was. "The school called me at work because they looked everywhere for you."

Emily looked down. She started to speak, then clamped her mouth shut. She repeated that sequence twice before squeaking out, "Hiding."

"Why? Who from? Where? No! Let's sit down first."

They sat at the kitchen table, Emily with a glass of juice, Katherine with a glass of Pinot Grigio. Emily explained the storeroom.

"You haven't been to recess since the second week of school?"

"No."

"So you don't know who is there or what has been happening, especially since Billy Medford was expelled?"

Emily shrugged. "After Billy left, most of the other seventh graders got friendly. They tell me what's going on in the afternoon."

"Dear, you don't have to hide now."

"I know, but Mom, you should see the place. No one has ever gone in there but me. I dusted and swept it, moved a nice leather chair in from another storeroom and a table for my lunch. I even built a bookcase from some orange crates."

"This is how you manage to read so many books?"
Emily nodded.

"Please, Mom, don't tell. I like it there. It's the only place in school where I can be alone, and I need that."

"Emily, you need to develop social skills on the playground too."

"I know." Emily hung her head and tried not to cry. "I need to be alone sometimes." Her eyes were glistening when she raised her head.

Katherine thought for a while. "You say that you can go either indoors or outdoors?" Emily nodded. "Let's try this. Keep track of the time, and halfway through recess, ease out among the others. Half a recess is better than none for those social skills. Does that sound like a plan?"

Emily nodded. "Why didn't they make an announcement? I would have heard that."

"Doctor Morgan wanted to talk to you, and said it was not urgent enough for an announcement. Go see her tomorrow."

"Yes, ma'am."

"And I never heard of this room." Katherine smiled.

THE LAST GOOD MAN?

KATHERINE HAMPSTEAD WAS WAITING OUT-
SIDE school when Emily came out pushing her bicycle.
Though the air was cold, the sun had shone for five days,
warming the streets and railroad tracks. Mother and
daughter were bundled for the cold air. Emily snapped her
book-bag pannier to her bicycle rack.

"Hi, Mom."

"How was school?"

"Fine."

Katherine arched her eyebrows. "All I get is a four-
letter word starting with F?"

"Really, Mom, it was fine. I can tell you about it at
home."

"Okay."

Mother and daughter enjoyed the commute each
day, but it had been the subject of their first argument
since moving to Newton last summer. After Christmas
break, Emily asked to ride her bike to school instead of
taking the bus.

"It's only two and a half miles, no farther than
Colonial Elementary in Fredericksburg.

"Emily, there are seven sets of tracks between here
and the school. It's too dangerous with all that traffic."

"Mom, I can cross railroad tracks, and Main Street has a wide shoulder. You've ridden there before."

"What's wrong with the bus? Are you still being bullied?"

"No. But I hate the diesel fumes, the waste of time, and the smell. Sitting at the bus stop when I could be in school already." She spread her hands and looked up at her mother. "Five miles per gallon and hours of idling. Want more?"

Her mother had ranted about fossil fuels for as long as Emily could remember. She even complained about having to use a car to commute to her job teaching literature at Wichita State University.

"I think I get it." Katherine looked out the window and sighed, as if thinking out details.

"Okay, but I'll ride with you."

"You haven't done that since second grade."

"I know, but there are too many unknowns here, for both of us. Besides, I'm bigger, so the drivers should see me easily." Emily had started growing, but she was still one of the shortest girls in seventh grade.

"What about snow and ice?"

"They don't have as many snow days here as they had in Virginia. I'll drop you off on my way to work. You'll have to walk home if I'm held up."

"Two and a half miles?"

"Got a problem? You're the one who hikes ten miles with a pack. Find out if you can use the bus for the return trip. It has to make the stops anyway."

Emily thought for a moment. Then she smiled.

"This will be more fun than the bus. Thanks, Mom."

"I must be nuts, but you're welcome."

***

Emily's phone rang as she and her mother walked into the kitchen after parking the bikes and closing the garage.

"Mark, why are you calling on my phone?"

Katherine put down the groceries and stared across the island.

"Because I want to ask your mother to the movies, but I have a hunch about it. Is she there?"

"Yes. Should I put this on speaker?"

"Sure."

Emily put the phone on the island.

"Well?" said Katherine.

"Hi, Katherine. Would you like to go to the movies Friday night? I'd like to see the new flick at the Chisholm Trail Theatre."

Emily gasped and put her hand to her mouth.

"I don't know, but someone else here seems to know what you're talking about. Emily?"

"*The Hunger Games*?"

Katherine could feel his grin on the line. He said, "See why I called Emily's phone?"

"Are you asking Emily for a date?"

"No, of course not. But could I face her later if you went and she missed it?"

"This is a threesome, I take it."

"If Emily wants to bring someone, it could be a foursome. Still on me. I want to see it."

"Have you read the book, Mark?"

"The whole series. Surprised?"

"Actually, I am. You're the first man I've met who would admit to reading YA novels."

"Collins writes well and I like awesome women. You know that. Emily, have you read the books?"

"Of course, Mark. I'm the target reader."

"Well, would you two like to go to the movies?"

"He's dating you, Mom. Better make up your mind."

"Of course, Mark. I'd love to. And I'll bring my chaperone, with or without her friend."

"Great. I'll pick you up at your place."

"Let's do dinner and a movie. Get tickets for the seven- or eight o'clock show and have dinner here before we go."

"Okay. See you Friday." He ended the call.

Katherine and Emily finished putting away the groceries.

"You didn't tell him that you read the books too, Mom."

"He didn't ask."

"This is like watching a ballet, you know."

"What do you mean?"

"You're attacking through his stomach, and he's wooing you through your daughter. Ever notice that?"

Katherine stopped folding the empty grocery bag. "I think you're right. Funny, isn't it? How do you feel about it?"

"I think it's fun. I like Mark."

"I'm glad. How much homework do you have?"

"None. We had a study hall last period."

"Want to ride?"

"Always." Emily was already heading for her room to change.

They rode out Hesston Road, which carried only local traffic because it paralleled Interstate 135. Speeding past Roadside Park, they turned west on 60th Street out to North Ridge Road, then south back to Newton. Twenty-four kilometers on Emily's bike computer.

Less than an hour later, they were back in the kitchen, stretching between gulps of protein shakes.

"One thing I can say about Kansas," said Emily. "I love being able to get up speed. There was always something to climb before."

"Me too. Those ravines at Middle Emma Creek are like speed bumps compared to Virginia."

"Mom, that wasn't fast for you. You're holding back, aren't you?"

"Not as much as I used to. You're getting faster, dear, and I sit in a car all day going to the University and back."

"Why didn't we get a place in Wichita?"

"Mostly the cost. I was able to buy the house here with a much smaller mortgage. I took a pay cut to come here."

"I didn't know that. Why did you do that?"

"I needed to move, Emily. Too many memories of your father, too many friends asking after me, which only kept reminding me."

"I think I know what you mean. But I traded in my friends for a bunch of bullies."

"I'm sorry about that, more than you know. I had no idea that would happen. Are you making any friends since the bullying stopped?"

"Kind of. Everyone is in cliques, you know, but at least they're all friendly now. And the girls in the Scout troop have been great."

"You're enjoying Girl Scouts, then?"

"Oh yes, especially this troop. I'm glad you let me join."

"You've been in the program since October, and you haven't sold me any cookies. Instead, I signed a release form for monthly campouts. Am I missing something?"

"Probably. This troop likes the outdoors. The other girls told me we'll learn sewing by fixing the clothes we ruin in the woods."

"What woods?"

"Yeah, I know what you mean. But I hear there are trees around Wilson Lake. Also, we're going to the Tallgrass Prairie National Preserve in April. They say the bison birth their calves then. It will be so cool."

"Do you miss Virginia?"

"At first, yes. But it hasn't been so bad since Christmas." Emily felt something deeper about the question. "What about you?"

"Same. But looking back, I realize that I haven't had a nightmare since we moved. Have you?"

Emily took in a sharp breath. "No. We both needed this move, didn't we?"

Katherine put her arms around her daughter. Emily snuggled in and sighed. "You don't miss Daddy?"

"Oh, I miss him. Badly. Every day. And I still cry easily when I think about it. But the terror of that day is slowly fading as we move on."

"What about Mark?"

"Mark helps me move on. For one thing, he seems to be deeply empathetic. I cried over Charlie one night. He held me and cried too."

"That's amazing."

"Yes. Unlike any man I've ever met. He feels deeply, and that's unusual. When Charlie comes up, I sense no jealousy at all. Mark wants to have his own place in our lives without displacing Charlie at all."

"He loves you, Mom."

"Yes, I think so."

"Do you love him?"

"I don't know. I want to, but then I get scared. When I met Charlie, I was convinced that there weren't any good men in this world. Then he showed me that there was at least one. Now I have to convince myself that he wasn't the last one out there." She looked at Emily with glistening eyes. "Does that make any sense to you?"

"Yes, but you just made me think that if Daddy was the last one out there, I'll be out of luck."

Katherine gasped and paused. "My God, Emily, what a thought." She squeezed her daughter. "Thank you."

K-BIKES

"HEY, MOM! LOOK AT THOSE BIKES." Emily pointed to a red SUV rolling out of the parking lot of Chisholm Middle School. On the roof were a pair of Colnago road racers. "Must be six thousand dollars on that car."

"Those are the smallest frames I've ever seen." Katherine shielded her eyes with her hand as they watched the SUV turn into the afternoon sun and drive away. "Do you think someone here rides them?"

"I don't know, but most of the other kids are bigger than I am."

"True. I guess an eighth-grade boy could ride those."

They clipped in and started their afternoon commute back to the house. Fifteen minutes later, they parked their bikes in the garage and shed their heavy winter clothing.

"I wonder if there's a racing team around here," said Emily as she pulled a pair of protein shakes from the refrigerator. She put one on the counter for her mother. "I'd like to try it."

"I never thought of that, but it would be fun, I'm sure." Katherine took a swig and looked out the window for a while. "I've got a clicking in my derailleur and my chain skips sometimes. Let me find a bike shop and we can start asking around."

"Already Googled it." Emily grinned as Katherine rolled her eyes. "K-Bikes downtown seems to be the only serious bike shop in town. They might have the kind of wrench you need." A wrench is a bicycle mechanic. "Want to ride there now?"

"Can we do it Saturday? I have papers to grade tonight."

"Okay."

Saturday morning, Emily and Katherine dismounted in front of the K-bikes store. The modern bike rack on the sidewalk, capable of taking a U-lock, was an encouraging sign.

Inside, the range of machines hanging on the walls and propped around the floor amazed them. A trim man with salt-and-pepper hair, and crow's feet from smiling, greeted them from the counter.

"Hello," said Katherine. "We're new in town, and I think I need my rear derailleur adjusted."

"We can handle that. Jake!"

A teenage boy came out from the back. Maybe eighteen years old, skinny, with dark hair and a pair of natural cowlicks. They stood and bent towards each other like the jaws of a wrench.

"Yes?" He reached up and twisted one cowlick with a greasy hand. Emily understood why they stuck out so well. She wondered if Jake were aware of his habit.

Katherine explained the problem. Jake hoisted the bicycle to his shoulder and set it on a work stand in the repair shop. He spun the chain, looked at the derailleur as he shifted gears, and checked the chain with a stretch gauge.

"You obviously take good care of your bike. I've never seen a chain this worn so well oiled. How long have you been riding with it?"

Katherine thought. "About five thousand kilometers, I think. I wasn't sure about getting an overhaul before we moved here in September."

Jake twisted the other stiff horn. "You need a new chain. This one will start putting shark's teeth on your chainrings and cogs. Were the brake cables new when you replaced the chain?"

"No. They might have eight thousand on them."

"Want to let me check some things while you shop around?"

"Sure. Thanks."

Emily smiled at Jake, who blushed. That surprised her. She had never had a boy blush at her before.

Out front, Emily joined her mother. The owner introduced himself as Matt Owens.

"Is there a racing team around here? I'd like to try road racing, but I don't know where to start."

"What grade are you?"

"Seventh."

"NICA has a middle school division, but there aren't any NICA teams around here." National Interscholastic Cycling Association.

"That's mountain biking anyway. I want to road race." Katherine raised her eyebrow. She had grown up competing on MTBs in Marin County. "I know, Mom. Where are the mountains around here?"

"We sponsor a USA Cycling team, but USAC starts in high school."

"Can I ride with you? I'm fast, but I'd like to learn how to ride with other racers."

"How fast?"

Emily looked at her mother. "Tell him, dear."

"I'm almost as fast as my mother," Emily said. "I guess we average thirty to forty kilometers per hour. It would be faster without traffic, of course."

"You're kidding!"

"That's what the bike computer shows. I don't know if it's real or not. That's partly why I want to ride with a team."

"What kind of bike do you have?"

Emily slapped her saddle. "This is it."

"A Bianchi Volpe?"

"It's my only bike, so it has to do everything. In Virginia, I had a cassette with smaller cogs put on it. Around here, I would be spinning like crazy otherwise."

Matt looked at Emily's gears. "That's a racing setup."

"I don't know about that, but it's more comfortable than what came on the bike."

Matt asked Katherine, "Did you know about this?"

"Just watched her grow. And one bike each is all we can afford, so she's right about having to make the Bianchi work."

Matt considered the two of them. They had the same auburn hair and hazel eyes. Full lips. Long lashes. The hard skinniness of seasoned bicyclists. No makeup. If Emily were any taller, they would look like sisters.

"And you've been riding that fast too?" He asked Katherine.

"Well, yes. I only stopped holding back this year. She's starting to grow and get faster."

Matt shook his head. He tapped a pencil on a pad by the cash register while he stared from one to the other.

"Why haven't I heard of you, Mrs. Hampstead?"

"Katherine, please. I dropped out of the pros when Emily came along. I wasn't USAC. I raced triathlons. And mountain bikes before NICA was a thing."

Jake came out, rolling Katherine's Pinarello. "Nice bike. I've never seen this model before."

"Thanks. It's been with me longer than Emily here."

"I put on a new chain. The derailleur is fine. I would get a tune-up and change out the cables soon. They look good, but with those miles on them, they could break at any time."

"How long do you need?"

"Two days, maybe."

"I'll come back with the car soon."

Matt thought silently while Jake took Katherine's credit card and rang up the sale for the chain.

Emily walked to the wall and admired a 46-cm Bianchi Volpe in the original celeste color. "This one is your size, Mom."

She glanced over before signing the credit card slip. "Probably your next bike, if you keep growing this year."

Matt snapped out of his thoughts.

"Emily," he said, "I should tell you to wait two years and come back, but, frankly, I have a hunch, and I'm excited that you want to learn with a real team. We train on Tuesday and Thursday afternoons starting at the High School parking lot. Do you know where it is?"

"Yes. We live near there."

"Normally we also race on Saturdays. The snow hasn't finished melting, or we'd be out there today. Can you do that?"

"I think so. It's okay if I can't race with the team yet."

"Good. I'll need you to sign some release forms and have your parents countersign."

"Can we sign now?"

Matt smiled at Katherine. "Is she always this confident?"

"Ask the eighth grader who pinched her butt."

"Omigod. Is that her?" The media had not released names of Emily or her assailant, but the incident on the school bus was still the talk of the coffee shops in town.

Katherine nodded. "And she only has the one parent, so we can do it here."

Fifteen minutes later, they paused at a red light on Main Street.

"Mom, this is going to be so much fun."

"Should I follow the team?" Emily scowled. Katherine laughed. "I'm not worried, but remember, it's different riding fast in a crowd. Do what Matt tells you."

Emily sighed. "Yes, Mom. Of course." Then she grinned. "Now that you have a new chain, let's ride out Hesston Road again." She blew through the green light as her mother stood on the pedals to catch up.

***

Tuesday afternoon, Emily rode to Newton High School from home. She recognized Matt lowering racing bikes from a K-Bikes van and handing them to a half-dozen teenagers. Some older riders were taking their bikes off their cars.

Seeing a twelve-year-old girl arrive on a city bike with racks, lights and fenders, the racers stopped to stare. Matt waved them together.

"This is Emily Hampstead." Matt pointed out the others, a fog of names that Emily would have to catch later. The stares had turned to curious looks. "She wants to learn how to race. Does anyone mind her tagging along today?"

"Coach, we were supposed to do sprints today." Tall, early twenties, black hair and beard, but shaved legs. "Do we have to do this?" The expressions on the others signaled their agreement that holding back for a little girl would not be fun.

"Who's taking her home?" asked a teenage girl with a shiny Colnago.

Matt tilted his head to Emily.

"No one," said Emily. "I'll go back the way I came." She slapped the saddle of her bike.

"Are you going to ride that?"

"Yes. Your bikes are all too big for me."

The girl shook her head.

"Okay? I told her that we won't hold back for her, and her mother agreed that she could ride home alone if she fell off the back."

"Same route as last week, coach?"

"No. Go out Twelfth Street to Burmac Road, then Grant to Hesston and back here on Meridian. Emily, can you remember that?"

"Sure. I've ridden that before. It's about sixty-five kilometers." That raised a few eyebrows.

"Right. And, like we agreed, just follow and watch. I'll answer questions after we get back."

"Thanks, coach."

"Everybody ready? Good. Pete, you take point until you cross Ridge Road. Trade up every five kilometers, first Myra, then Jack then whoever is next at that point. Everyone takes a turn – except Emily here, of course.

After each change, sprint for five hundred meters. Got it? I want to see some smooth shifting in the pack. Let's go." He walked back to the van, while the others rolled out in a line behind Pete.

Emily fell in behind the last rider, a boy who smiled weakly at Emily as he started out. She kept about ten meters behind him. *This distance should not worry anyone.* She was not sure what to make of the cool reception, but then, her mother had warned her that these would be jocks, not inclined to welcome what they would see as a little girl with silly dreams. She didn't care; she was here to watch.

The sun was weak in the winter sky, but it felt good on Emily's face as they rode towards it. Emily watched with interest as the riders adjusted position every five kilometers. The lead rider would pull to the left and coast, allowing the peloton to pull up before falling in at the end. She had read about drafting, which involved riding in the slipstream of another rider. It cut wind resistance for the following rider, without causing any increase in effort for the leader. Taking turns riding in front, a peloton could ride at high speed all day.

Emily had tried it with her mother, but Katherine was nervous about it. Drafting was not a skill she had developed on mountain bikes or in triathlons. Emily found it fascinating, and she hoped this team would let her stay, so she could master it.

Drafting may help the peloton increase its speed, but the ride was not particularly challenging for Emily. During the five-hundred-meter sprints, she got up to a comfortable pace, but then the whole line slowed down for the next four and a half kilometers.

The sun was setting as they pulled into the parking lot at Newton High School.

Pete, who was the one who had questioned the coach and led the ride out, came back to meet her.

"Emily, that's impressive. I can't believe you kept up with us."

Emily shrugged. "I ride a lot. I just have never done it with others, except my mom."

"Ready to take point?"

"Huh?"

"Take the lead."

"Oh, no. That trading off was fascinating. I've never seen drafting in person. But I want to watch some more first, please. This was fun."

Pete laughed. "Of course. We'll let the coach make that call."

Matt appeared. "Good idea. Want a lift home, Emily?"

"No, thanks. I live just over there." She pointed to the neighborhood beyond the fence.

"Okay. See you Thursday?"

"Sure!" She reached down and switched on her blinking lights. "Bye."

Half the other riders smiled and waved as she moved smoothly across 12th Street and turned left.

***

It was clear after four rides that they were not going to leave Emily behind. They were getting back to the parking lot at least an hour before sunset, as the days lengthened, and everyone's fitness grew out of the winter doldrums. Just before the first day of spring, Matt waved the team into a circle.

"I didn't expect Emily to keep up like this. Are we ready to let her join the peloton?"

"Isn't that your call, coach?" asked Myra.

"Not really. It's tight in there. You all have to work together. If anyone is concerned about Emily being in the pack, let's not do it."

The cyclists looked at each other.

"Could I just draft off the back at first?" asked Emily. "I would drop back on each change then draft the new tail rider."

"I like it," said Pete. "She wouldn't be in the middle of a mishap, but she could start learning to draft before joining the peloton."

"Okay," said Matt. "Let's try it. Saturday is a training ride. No race. Will everybody be here?"

***

"Mom, drafting is just so cool! It was like taking a break for two hours. I didn't even break a sweat until the last mile."

Katherine smiled. She was straddling her Pinarello, having ridden up to meet the team coming back to the parking lot.

"I knew that you were very steady on your bike. Was anyone worried that you would bump them?"

"If they were, they didn't say anything. And I was careful not to overlap anyone's wheel."

"Good." She waved at Matt. "Enough for today, or would you like to let out the stops?"

"I'll show you our route today. It's new. Let's go!" Emily waved at the team and swung onto her bike. As Katherine stood on her pedals to catch up, most of the team stopped to stare at the girl flying out 12th Street into the distance.

Riding together after the Saturday ride became a routine for Katherine. Emily could not participate in the races, so on away race days, they would ride to destinations around Newton: Hutchinson, Cottonwood Falls, and the tourist attractions in Wichita. After realizing how far they were riding, Katherine started commuting to Wichita State University whenever she had no morning classes, which was twice a week this semester.

In April, Mark joined them on their Saturday rides. He had also started using his bike to go to work a few times each week, which allowed him to gain the kind of fitness he needed to ride with Katherine and her daughter.

"I know you two are holding back for me," he said on the third Saturday. "I don't want to ruin your training."

"It's for fun, Mark," said Emily. "I don't mind taking it easy, especially now that the team has integrated me into the peloton."

"Let me guess: you're pulling them," said Katherine.

"When it's my turn to lead, but I'm not sure anyone notices, because they're drafting. Of course, on the sprints, it's another story, but they're getting used to that."

"I'll bet Matt wishes he could lie about your age," said Mark.

"Maybe, but I'm enjoying this as it is."

***

Emily closed the door on the dishwasher and turned it on. Katherine dried out the pasta pot and put it in the cabinet.

"Has Mark popped the question yet?"

"What question?"

"Doh! 'Do you want to come up and see my etchings?'" She wiggled her eyebrows.

"Emily Marian Hampstead, shame on you!" She snapped the dish towel at her daughter.

Emily jumped back and laughed. "I mean, if you look at the time he spends with us, the guy can't have any social life. He's been in love with you since before I met him."

"Maybe he's too much of a gentleman."

"That and maybe you intimidate him. The troop is camping out next weekend. Maybe you should bring him home."

"Emily!"

Emily laughed again. She picked up her French textbook and turned to go to her room. "Well, if he wants to propose, don't tell him you have to check with me. I'm fine with it."

She left her mother sitting at the kitchen table thinking deeply about the wisdom of children and how they see some things more clearly than grown-ups.

NIGÅ ANSWERS QUESTIONS

EMILY HAMPSTEAD HEARD HER MOTHER walking around downstairs. She had never known Katherine Dempsey to pace, especially from room to room. Katherine called up the stairs.

"Emily, do you have your grandmother's books?" Louise Massey had been a linguistic anthropologist, best known for her work on the Indigenous peoples of the East Coast of North America.

Emily closed her geometry textbook. *Oops! I didn't think she'd notice.* She walked to the landing.

"Which one? I have the Algonquian dictionary here."

"I could swear all three books of the Contact series were in the living room. But they're gone, and her other books are pushed over to close the place where they were."

"I'm sorry, Mom. I took them before you got home one day. I forgot to ask about it."

"Oh, good." Katherine paused. "Have you suddenly taken an interest in the Algonquin?"

"I wanted to know more about Gramma and Great-Gramma, and I got caught up in the story. Gramma Louise's books are really interesting."

"They are. So, how many books do you have? I'd like to check something in Volume One and something else in Volume Three."

"Uh, all of them." Emily twisted her hands, a habit her mother recognized.

"Emily, where are they?"

"At school." She shut her mouth hard and looked at her feet.

"I hope you mean that reading room I'm not supposed to know about." Emily had created a private space in an abandoned storage room when in the seventh grade. She'd outfitted it with a chair, a table for her lunch, and bookcases made from orange crates. It was where she hid and read for half of recess every day. Her mother had not mentioned it since then.

"Yes, ma'am. I'll bring them back tomorrow."

"Please do. Those books are out of print. If we lose any, we can't just order a new one easily."

"Oh, I didn't realize that."

"Now you know." Katherine motioned to the kitchen. Emily followed her in. "That's pretty heavy reading for middle school. What have you read?"

"Everything. I was keeping the Contact books because I like to go back and check them against what we read in our history class."

Katherine poured some juice for each of them. They sat at the kitchen table.

"I hope you're not challenging Mrs. Henderson with what you've learned."

"Oh, no! That would risk the other kids finding out about us. But it is annoying to see some of the garbage in our history texts. It's flat wrong, even using their own sources. There are books in the library that contradict the textbook."

"You're learning to read like a scholar, Emily. That's good. It's also surprising at your age."

"It's interesting when it's this personal. Gramma and Great Gramma told me that it's a special secret, so I've never breathed a word."

"Goodness, sweetheart. You were only four at my parents' funeral."

"I know. But Nigå set me up on a chair in the living room in the big house in the Marsh to tell me. It's almost the only memory I have of her. She looked in my face with such a serious expression, that I would die before I let anyone know."

Katherine chuckled. "She was right." Emily arched her eyebrows in a question. "Nigå Marian told me how we get our youngest children to be discrete about the Ninnuok. You've been keeping the secret all these years?"

Emily nodded. She wondered if she had done something wrong. "Is it really a secret?"

"No, dear. But now you're thirteen, and I can explain. What differences have you noticed between us and the Indigenous Americans in your history books?"

"The others are on reservations. But you and Gramma told me that none of us live on reservations. Also, the people on the reservations seem to be very poor and have lots of problems. I don't think they made a very good deal with the government."

"Have you read about our organizational structure, such as it is?"

"The Algonquin tribes, especially the Abenaki and the Penacook, are patrilineal, but the Ninnuok are matrilineal. In our history book, they only mention the male chiefs and the tribes with patriarchal structures.”

“Very observant, dear. Why do you think the Pawtucket ‘disappeared’ from the record after the epidemic of 1633?” She put air quotes on the verb.

They sat silently, while the girl pondered this thought.

“The colonists would have made them set up a patriarchal system like the other tribes.”

“Right. In other words, we would have suffered the same fate as the Wampanoag, the Massachusett, and the Abenaki, at least here in the US. We would have been reorganized out of existence. Your six- or seven-times great grandmother was the saunksqua in 1633. Only a few women of the Bear totem survived the epidemic. They came back from the praying town where they had taken refuge and settled in the Marsh, which had been our ancestral lands for millennia. The white men never went there, and no one paid attention to women. So they maintained the Ninnuok until the present.”

“It’s not a secret?”

“Not really. But there is no recognized tribe, and it is more convenient for everyone to keep it that way. We try not to discuss it with outsiders. Can you imagine trying to explain our system to the Bureau of Indian Affairs?”

“I read about that in Volume Two. Just the idea of the woman proposing and being free to divorce her husband without a court hearing would have driven everyone nuts.”

“The saunksqua today is in contact with women in forty-five states, and they continue to check in, especially when considering getting married. We try to pick men who will be equal, supportive partners.”

"What about the men?"

"We've had less than dozen sågamåk over the last three hundred years. There's no prohibition against it, but few of them are interested in the job."

"I think it is interesting that the language has no distinction between genders, just animate and inanimate. Makes it hard to translate, though." Emily collected their glasses and put them in the dishwasher. "Why haven't you ever talked to me about all this?"

"For one thing, we weren't living in the Marsh. We were living in Fredericksburg, so it was hard to build a connection. I'm glad Nigå scared you like she did, because I wondered what I would do when you started asking questions. Instead, you've gone off and read the answers on your own."

"Why do you need to see those two books now?"

"I have some ideas for a book or two of my own, and I wanted to check some of the things my mother wrote."

"What about the history of military nursing?"

"Still editing and revising, but the research and drafting is behind me. I'm thinking of a story about the Dawn People, and I wanted to check some things to see if my idea would fit."

"A historical novel?"

"Yes."

"That would be so cool. May I read it?"

"Of course, dear, but I won't have anything to show you for years. Historical fiction can take more research than nonfiction sometimes."

"That's okay. I'm sure it will be a bestseller."

Katherine tousled Emily's hair. "That's sweet. Mark will be here in a half hour, and I want to change before our three-way date."

"Me, too." She started the dishwasher and followed her mother, both of them whistling the theme from *The Hunger Games.*

KINÅBA

EMILY FLUSHED THE TOILET and stared at her panties. Her mother was singing in the kitchen.

"Mom, I may have started my period." She heard the crash of a pan hitting the floor.

"Be right there!" Footsteps. Katherine opened the door. "Let's see."

They examined the tiny spots together.

"The color looks different from a cut, I think," Emily said.

"It is." Katherine reached into the cabinet under the sink. "Here. You could ignore such a small amount but put this inside a fresh pair. Breakfast is almost ready." She gave Emily a panty liner, then returned to the kitchen.

They ate in silence, often staring out the window at the clear sunshine of a Monday morning.

"Last week of school for you, Mom."

"Exams and grading. With your finals next week, we'll finish up together this year." Katherine took a bite of scrambled eggs.

Emily sipped some juice. "What's wrong, Mom? You look sad."

"Not sad, just thinking. It hits parents when their children grow up."

"Oh. Yeah. I guess. I mean, it had to happen sometime, didn't it?"

"Of course. And we always think we're ready, until another milestone like this comes along." Katherine smiled, then looked beyond Emily's shoulder again.

They finished in silence, then loaded the dishwasher, and got ready for their morning commute: Emily to Chisholm Middle School, Katherine to Kansas State University in Wichita. They had stopped riding to the middle school together in April, when Emily had grown tall enough to be seen easily on her bike. This was one of those mornings when they both missed their old commute.

That afternoon, they rolled their bikes into the garage about the same time.

"Mom, when does summer school start at the University?"

"The middle of June, but I don't have to teach this year."

"Wow! You've, like, *never* had the summer off."

"I know. It was one of the deals I made with Dean Shanholtz. I don't start teaching summers until next year." This was Katherine's first year teaching at KSU.

"Omigod, we could do a real vacation."

"I've been thinking about that, but let's discuss it inside."

Showered, changed, and sitting in the living room, Katherine looked seriously at her daughter.

"What would you like to do besides Scout camp this year?"

"I'd give that up for a long ride. You know, touring and camping. Visit a National Park. Ride one of the great trails, like the OTET," (Ohio to Erie Trail) "or the Erie Canal."

"You think we could camp for more than a weekend?"

"Why not? We have the gear, and you know we can ride the miles, even with loaded bikes."

"What about the K-bikes team?"

"I get my USAC card next year." USA Cycling. "This could be my last summer before I join the racing circuit. It may be our only chance for years to do a long tour."

"I agree. It scares me a little. I've never roughed it for so long."

"How hard can it be if we stick to the roads and bike trails?" Emily rose and walked to the file cabinet where they kept the maps. She pulled out a AAA map and the book from the Adventure Cycling Association. "Let's see."

"Where would you like to go?"

"Everywhere. Here. Look at all these great rides." Emily's finger tapped the colored lines on the map of the United States. "The TransAmerica Trail here in Newton, the Eastern Express Connector, the Underground Railroad, the Katy Trail, the Freedom Trail, the OTET, the Northern Tier, the Erie Canal Trail, the Empire Trail. Mom, with a whole summer we can go *anywhere*."

"Any destination in particular, dear?"

"I don't care. It's all about the ride, isn't it?" Emily paused and considered her mother's face, the eyes looking at the Northeast. "Mom, I've seen that look. Where do *you* want to go?"

Katherine looked up. "The Marsh, *Kzihla*." (She Runs Fast).

"Yes! That would be so cool. I could see Patty and my other cousins."

"But do we have time?" They looked at the map. Emily muttered under her breath as she used her fingers as a compass.

"I reckon five weeks or less to get there if we ride all the way." She dragged her finger over the route. "And look at all the great trails." She looked up at her mother. "Could we afford to take the train back, so we can ride the whole thing?"

"I did check into round trip train travel to Rowley last week. We have our home in the Marsh when we get there. So, yes, we can use the train to make it work. I just don't know about lodging along the way. Even the campgrounds and parks are not free."

"Warmshowers?" A social network for bicycle tourists, hosting and guesting.

"That would help. I'll look into it. We should expect to host others coming through when we get back. Newton *is* on the TransAmerica Trail."

"Then we could meet some of those riders. I'll bet they have some great stories to tell."

"Something else, dear." Katherine smiled wistfully. "I called the sågamå this morning. We would be arriving for the Blueberry Moon – late July. Do you know what happens then?" Emily shrugged. "*Wizwågan.*"

"The name?" Emily thought. "The Naming Ceremony. I've never seen that."

"Because only the grown-ups attend. It is time for you to receive your final name."

"Isn't my name Kzihla? You always called me that in private."

"Yes, because you were so fast as a little one. You still are. If we go, though, the sachem would discern a new name for you, by which you would be known the rest of your life."

"Let's go! This will be so exciting."

"Better than *Star Trek?*"

"We'll set out boldly," Emily imitated the announcer on the TV show. She gave her mother a hug. "Let's make some notes about what we need that we don't have." They moved to Katherine's study, booted up the computer and looked at checklists for camping and touring.

*****

In late June, they camped at the Cuyahoga National Park south of Cleveland. In the end, only Katherine needed to buy something: a decent sleeping bag. One of Emily's Girl Scout friends lent them her older brother's lightweight tent. Katherine's Pinarello was a road racing bike, but it was built when steel frames were stronger on racing bikes, so she was able to outfit it with racks and 28-mm tires. It handled fine.

"Warmshowers message from Glenn." Their host in Cleveland. Emily tapped her phone. "He says we must plan on seeing the Museum of Art and Heinen's Grocery Store."

"A grocery store?"

"I Googled it. It's a landmark."

"Oookayy." Katherine took the rice pilaf from the fire and served it on their mess kits.

"We've already seen all kinds of things I never knew about. The blue cheese at the Amish market in Berlin was worth the trip. Let's mail-order some when we return home."

"And learning about the wine club from Marie in Akron."

An elderly couple stopped at their campsite and invited them to join them for a cold drink. They accepted.

"That's the third time, we've been welcomed to someone else's beer or wine," said Katherine. "These campers are a friendly bunch."

"Maybe we should get something to contribute, if this will be a trend."

"Glass is heavy."

"Well, beer in cans doesn't weigh much."

"But you have to drink it warm like the English. We don't have a cooler." Katherine took a towel and began drying the plates and pans that Emily had washed. "For now, let's be grateful. I think they enjoy doing it regardless."

The next day, it rained. Hard. The Cuyahoga Trail (part of the OTET) turned to a muddy mess so they had to push their bikes up to the road and ride on the asphalt. Better quality rain gear went on their growing Christmas list as they pedaled into Cleveland. The sun came out just as they turned onto the street where their host lived.

***

Emily and Katherine stood by their bikes outside the diner in Georgetown, Massachusetts. The day had been hot, but mostly cloudy, so their sunblock had lasted.

"Only about twenty kilometers now," said Emily. "We could be fixing supper at home."

"Funny how you say 'home' when we only come here for holidays."

"Home is where you park your wheels." Emily slapped her saddle.

Katherine smiled. "Well, it has been for the last month, hasn't it? Have we really crossed half the continent in that time?"

"You're awesome, Mom. No one else I know could have covered as much ground as we have."

They swung onto their bikes and rolled the last hour to the end of Town Farm Road, just past the county transfer station. The dirt trail that led into the Wildlife Management Area was soft from the rain that week, so they pushed their steeds the last mile to the house. As they rounded the last turn on the trail, they both stopped.

The house stood tall in the Marsh, two stories above a wraparound porch that rested on stilts holding it at least ten feet above the ground. The windows were all closed, the white drapes drawn, which meant that the house would not have heated up inside. They leaned their bikes against the front porch and shed their muddy shoes. Katherine got out her key and let them in.

The shady interior felt cool after the muggy ride from Georgetown.

"Someone has been here." Emily checked the refrigerator and took out a half gallon of cold orange juice. "There's enough food in here for days."

"Niben probably turned on the power after I called her yesterday." Katherine put out two glasses. "Another nice thing about having a home. Family who can check on it. Remind me to pay her bill at the store. She would refuse if I were to try to pay her back."

"Isn't Niben your cousin?"

"Her husband, John Hawkins."

"The sågamå?"

"Yes. I'll call them while you take your panniers upstairs."

An hour later, they were showered, changed, and setting the table in the kitchen. Katherine took the roast potatoes out of the oven, while Emily served up the salmon filets and broccoli.

Supper was never a rushed affair in their family. They ate quietly, each thinking of the wonderful sights they had seen, and enjoying the pleasure of a meal cooked at home. John had told Katherine that they might come by tomorrow to welcome them personally.

"I hope I don't get a dorky name." Emily speared a piece of broccoli and chewed slowly.

"From what Nigåk Louise and Marian told me, no one ever gets a dorky name. The sachem nails it every time."

"But they don't even know me here."

"Emily, the Ninnuok are spread all over the country. Some only come back for funerals and the Wizwågan."

"Where do they stay? There are only a few expensive B&Bs around here."

"With kin. I remember some staying in this house, the summer I was named."

"Wait a minute. You told me you all stayed away until you were, what, eighteen?"

"My freshman year in college. That was when my mother made up with my grandmother. I asked to join the Ninnuok, and I received my name between my freshman and sophomore years."

"You've never mentioned that. *Wawinlewa?*" (What is your name?)

"*Nikånka.*" (She Who Races Ahead).

"That fits you." Emily took a sip of her water. "I still hope I don't get a dorky name."

***

205

Emily lashed the walking stick to the rack of her bike and wheeled it out of the shed. The ground was dry today, so she mounted up and rode to the asphalt of Town Farm Road, her tires kicking dust into the cool air of a dawning day. Her cousin Patty Hawkins was waiting outside their modest home in the woods near Lufkin Creek when Emily rode up. She stood as tall as Katherine, with the same broad shoulders and erect bearing of generations of Massey women. Her black hair was braided down her back. She wore trekking clothes and a baseball cap.

"Hey, *Pitålo*! Why so early? The sun is barely up."

"I hope you remember not to call me that where others can hear."

"Oh. Sorry. Your real name is so cool, though. Mountain Lion. Grrr!"

Patty tousled her hair. "All our names are cool. And I have the claws to go with it." She flexed her perfectly manicured fingers to show off the reinforced pearlescent nails.

"Omigod, that's fabulous! Where did you have that done?"

"I did the prepping myself, so Judy – remember her? – could do the painting and drying at Main Street Nails for half-price."

"You could be deadly with those."

"Well, I'd rather save them and use my elbows. To answer your question, if we want to be coasting downhill in the heat of the day instead of hiking uphill, we need to leave early. You ready?"

"Sure. I even remembered to bring a walking stick."

Patty gasped slightly. "Where did you get that stick, Em?"

"It was in the closet by the door."

"You can't carry that. It belongs to the sågamå."

"Oh. You mean it's your father's stick?"

"No. Whoever is the sågamå or saunksqua carries it. And only when they are in office. Dad gets it from your house when he needs it."

"I didn't know that."

"Here. Let's put it inside, and I'll lend you my brother's stick. We can put it back this evening."

With sticks switched, they mounted up and rode to Halibut Point State Park on Cape Ann. After locking their bikes, they hiked the trails around Babson Farm Quarry. They took photos and selfies at the quarry, and at the Ocean Viewpoint. On such a clear day, Mount Agamenticus in Maine was visible behind the Isles of Shoals in New Hampshire.

After a picnic on the rocks at the Halibut Point Reservation, they hiked back to the bikes and blasted their way back to Essex, stopping for ice cream on the way. Emily retrieved the saunksqua stick and hugged her favorite cousin.

"Thank you for standing for me next week, Pitålo," Emily, looking around as she theatrically stretched out Patty's name. "I know almost no one here, and this means so much to me."

"As it should. I can tell by your talking that Katherine has schooled you well."

"As well as she could. It's just the two of us in Kansas, but we do have Nigå Louise's books to help."

"Oh, yes. I saw those in Dad's office. I want to read them now. See what Mom got wrong." They chuckled.

With a hug and an arm squeeze, Emily was off. She rolled up to the house in the Marsh just as her mother was unsnapping her panniers.

"Just in time to help with supper. How's Patty?"

***

Emily looked up from the book she was reading when her mother came in with a clothing bag neatly folded in her arms. Katherine's eyes were glistening. Again. *She's done a lot of that this week*, the girl thought.

"Are you excited about tomorrow?"

"Yes, Mom. I was just re-reading the descriptions in Volume One of the Contact series."

"Have you thought about what to wear?"

"I have the buckskin outfit that we keep here, and those fantastic moccasins you gave me this morning. Won't that be okay?"

"Sure, but try this." She unzipped the bag and took out a tunic and a pair of trousers. Buttons carved from oyster shells shone with pearlescent purple. The stitching was flawless. No label in the neck to tell where it came from.

"Mom, this is so soft! It's beautiful. Where did you get it?"

"It's mine, but now it will be yours. Your grandmother and your great-grandmother wore it. Her mother made this."

"Omigod. The one who built this house?"

"Yes. Amazing woman. A legend among the Ninnuok."

"Will it fit me?"

"You may have noticed that we are all the same size as adults. It was tight on me at eighteen, but my mother said that it fit her and Nigå Marian just fine when they were your age. It's deerskin, so it will stretch some if it needs to. Try it on."

They walked upstairs, Emily holding the package like a monstrance in a sacred procession. Her heart pounded, as her head ran the numbers. *This is ninety years old! It's an artifact. I can't do this!*

"How have you kept it in such good condition?"

"Deerskin wears well, but also, Nigåk Ethel in Gloucester and Almira in Rockport know the old ways of caring for it."

"Is that Pitålo's Aunt Ethel who runs the dry cleaner?" Katherine nodded. "Still, it is almost a hundred years old."

"Like wedding gowns and Communion dresses, this has only been worn three times. Nigå Marian made it available to the People for their girls, but no one took her up on it. Every mother wants her daughter to have a special garment for Wizwågan. Even the poorest families manage to make or buy something, or pass something down through generations, like this."

Emily changed while her mother sat at the table, holding back her tears. As Emily turned to the mirror after pulling her ponytail out, she ran her hands down the front of the shirt. She felt the souls of her ancestors warming her, protecting her.

"Oh, Mom, it fits like a glove." Overcome, she ran into her mother's arms. They hugged for a long time.

"Let's not get it wet." Katherine wiped her eyes. Emily stood back. She changed back into her jeans, then carefully hung the garment in her closet.

***

The next morning while Emily and Katherine were pulling the dining table to the wall, someone knocked on the front door. Emily went to it. A tall lady stood there, dressed in light blue skirt and blouse. Silver hair tied back in a long braid, like Emily remembered her grandmother. Face weathered from many years outdoors, but the crows' feet were from much smiling. Her expression seemed severe now, however, and she gripped a *mdåkwat* in her left hand, like a weapon. Emily recognized the medicine stick from illustrations in her grandmother's books, and she suppressed a gulp.

"*Kwai, Nigå,*" she said, then bowed slightly and stepped back, opening the door fully. "*Aquène. Ponåmuk.*" (Peace. Come in.)

Katherine came into the hall. "Oh, Susan. It's so good to see you."

The older woman smiled at Emily and said to Katherine in Pawtucket. "You have done well, Nikånka." Emily blushed. Katherine took the hint and switched languages.

"She made it easy, Kzighilo. This is my daughter Kzihla. Thank you for coming. I would feel much better knowing that we are setting up correctly."

For the next hour, Kzighilo (Susan Hawkins to outsiders) went over the preparations, helping Emily and Katherine move furniture, checking the recipes for the summer squash soup that they would serve, and the arrangements for babysitting upstairs. They had stocked food, drinks, snacks, and games in the guest room, which had a kitchenette and a water closet. Two older teenagers, friends of Patty Hawkins, had volunteered to run the nursery.

The sachem stayed for a light lunch, then left. She would be back with her adult relatives later.

***

By sundown, the downstairs was "standing room only." More than three dozen people chatted comfortably, as they waited for the noise upstairs to settle down. Emily learned that they had brought their children, either to participate if of age, or to play and sleep upstairs if not.

Almost everyone was wearing buckskin clothing, though some had dress shirts and their best trousers. The front porch was littered with dozens of moccasins and a few sneakers. Two pair of work boots.

Emily sought out the others coming of age. One girl, Abby, was a second cousin or something. The three boys came from two families that lived near the Penacook in New Hampshire: Peter, Jeremiah, and Walter.

When the teenager signaled from the stairs, the sachem moved to the table. She spread her arms, and held them out, while the adults moved against the walls to create a space for the twelve- and thirteen-year-olds to gather in the middle. Pitălo stood behind Kzihla; a different adult stood behind each of the others.

Kzighilo opened with the Thanksgiving Prayer, then the prayer for a Quest. She addressed the candidates in Pawtucket, but the stares of the three boys made it obvious that they could not follow.

"How much can you understand?" she asked them in English.

"I think most of it," said Peter, "but I miss important words, and I can't follow that fast."

"Then we will go slowly, until your mothers can help you learn." She looked at the two sets of parents across the room. "Meanwhile, feel free to answer in Penacook or Abenaki if you can. They're close enough."

She asked them to describe what they did for their vision quest and what they learned. Each of the three boys had undertaken to hike alone with a small pack from Seabrook to Bear Brook State Park, camp, then hike back, some forty miles each way.

"I thought I would sleep all night, I was so exhausted," said Peter using a mix of Penacook, Pawtucket, and English, "but the pains in my leg kept me awake. I learned I need to think ahead to do something like this. I could not even start a fire because I forgot matches."

"*Mosa?*" (Moose)

"I was surprised to learn how much stuff I could have left behind," said Jeremiah. "I managed to make a trap and caught a rabbit."

The sachem looked at Walter.

"I also forgot many small things," he said, "but I was able to improvise using what I found and my knife. That made me worry, but then I felt good."

"*Pemega?*" (She Dances).

Abby looked at Emily, then at the sachem.

"I was going to take my canoe to the Merrimack River," she said in Pawtucket, "then to Lawrence."

"That is a long trip, in a very busy part of the river."

"I know, but it would test more than just my endurance to work past the traffic safely, and to camp along the way."

"What did you learn?"

"That plans fall apart quickly. Two boys on jet skis harassed me at Newburyport and capsized my canoe. They were gone by the time I righted it and pulled it ashore. I was able to get to Maudslay State Park after dark, and camp there. The next morning, I saw an otter floating in the river. He had a gunshot wound in his shoulder, but he was still alive. I brought him aboard and paddled to the Whalen Wildlife Rescue in Haverhill. They said I did all the right things, and they let me watch them set his shoulder. I helped bandage him and set food out for him. The sun had set, so I spent the night in Groveland with one of the volunteers, then returned to the Marsh the way I came. Lawrence will have to wait for another day."

"Let me see your hands."

Abby held out her hands. Kzighilo rubbed the palms with her thumbs, then looked at both sides of the girl's hands carefully.

"Kzihla?"

Emily had been dreading this since learning yesterday that this sachem made the youth share their quest. She was not sure riding somewhere with her mother would count.

"I'm sorry, but I did not do my quest alone. I rode here from Newton, Kansas, to experience the many wonders. It took us a month in all kinds of weather, but I did not suffer. I learned to be grateful for the kindness of strangers, because we encountered that in so many ways on our journey."

The sachem seemed surprised. She turned to Katherine.

"Nikånka, whose idea was this?"

"Hers, Nigå. I had planned to take the train."

"Kzilå, would you have done this alone?"

"In a flash! I had always wanted to ride those long routes." She blushed and looked at her mother. "Sorry."

"You're the one who set out boldly. I was terrified."

The sachem turned to the table and picked up a bowl of dark liquid that she had prepared before everyone arrived. It was thick, like melted chocolate, but it had a reddish hue and a sharp smell.

She gave the bowl to each young person to sip from, then she prayed over each, with her hands on their heads. She went in the order that they had told their stories.

"*Keme.*" Thunder. She had chosen the basic Algonquian form, so the boy understood. He smiled.

"*Tmakwa.*" Beaver. "Because you make things." Jeremiah also grinned.

"*Nojikat*" Builder. "Because you will make what the people need."

To Abby, she said, "*Wlimliki.*" Gentle and Strong.

Last, she gave the bowl to Emily.

"*Taguagualokamu?*" Emily asked. (Shall I finish it?)

Kzighilo smiled and shook her head. "*Nda.*" Emily took a sip. It was bitter, but like an adult drink, maybe a beer with too many hops.

While Emily held the bowl, the sachem placed her hands on Emily's head. She prayed, then said,

"*Kinåba.*" Bold One.

RESENTMENT

MY NAME IS WILLIAM MEDFORD. No middle name. 'Billy' to most people before Emily Hampstead happened to me. She has a middle name, but I don't know what it is. Don't care. I hate that girl, but when I'm sober and thinking straight, I admit she not only saved my life; she redeemed it.

I wasn't looking forward to sophomore year at Newton High School, but it was better than home schooling, which is what I had to do for eighth grade. And being back in public school meant that I could take driver's ed. Otherwise, I would never have got my license, which I did the summer I turned sixteen.

That summer I also grew big enough to beat up Pop the last time he hit my mother. He wasn't my father, but until that summer, I had to go hide somewhere when he came back from Smokey's Bar or whatever job he'd just been fired from. The alternative was ducking blows myself.

When he got up, he went to their bedroom, packed a bag, and left. Good riddance. I never heard from him again, but Stevie who works at Smokey's said he got arrested for trying to rob the place.

The bruises on my hands healed quickly. I got a job washing dishes at the pizzeria next to Smokey's. Who knew they would have so many dishes? I thought everything was in cardboard pizza boxes. They paid cash at the end of the day, so no stupid paperwork. Not much money, but it put gas in the truck and paid for my books for school. Tony was a good boss: he let me have Friday nights off for football games, and I could work either Saturday or Sunday if I let him know by Wednesday.

Mom went to the welfare office and got a WIC or EBT card, or something, so we had food. My father's life insurance paid off the mortgage, so we had the house.

Mom got her old job back as a waitress at the diner near our house. She didn't make the kinds of tips she used to before Pop made her quit, but between us, we could make it. She was still pretty good-looking for her age, but ten years of getting beat up and living with an asshole shows after a while. She had the spiel and the smile, though. Sometimes I would sit in the corner with a Coke just to watch her for a while. The customers really enjoyed having her wait on them. I know Buddy, the owner, was pleased. I was proud of my mom.

For a while, life was good. I had my mom. I had my gang at school. I played football. I wasn't as fast or as heavy as the coach wanted, but I made second-string lineman, and that got me dates with the better chicks. Being anything on the football team was better than being a nerd or a doofus.

And I had the truck. It wasn't new: my father bought it, so it was almost as old as I was. I washed it every week and waxed it every month. It was green, which was good, because the red trucks I saw around town all lost their paint in the sun. I was good under the hood, so I could fix anything that needed fixing. Mr. Curtis, our shop teacher, ran a garage south of town, and he said I could get a full-time job there after high school if I wanted. His company would even pay for the SAE classes and certification.

Mom didn't like to drive, so she was happy when I got my license and could take her places: church, Wichita Gardens, Chisholm Trail Center for the shopping or the movies.

Only one thing bothered me as a successful, good-looking football jock with his own truck: Emily Hampstead. We were on the same bus at Chisholm Middle School when she arrived in seventh grade. I was a year ahead of her, and two years older, so she was a short, scrawny kid to me. But she was cute, with that dark red-gold hair they call auburn. The second day she boarded the bus, I squeezed her butt as she went by. She slapped me, but I fixed that by twisting her arm. The other kids thought it was hilarious, so I made a point of pinching her butt every day.

Until she got on the bus one Monday and dislocated my elbow. What the fuck? The school didn't do anything because she had turned in a complaint on me and her fancy mother from Wichita State had filed a complaint, too.

For a month, I kept trying to get even, but she was never at recess, and I couldn't do anything in the crowd going to the bus. My posse was useless. We beat up the kids who wouldn't rat on her, but looking back, I don't think they knew where she went when she wasn't in class. The third time I was suspended for hitting someone at recess, they expelled me. Some bullshit about being the first expulsion in the history of the school. I spent the rest of eighth grade at home, with Mom trying to go through the lesson plans with me. We both hated it.

For whatever legal reason, I could go to Chisholm High School. And there she was. Only now she was taller than me. Still kind of thin, but she had a swagger and a tilt to her head that I always noticed. I could tell when she was coming down the hall before she rounded the corner. There was this vibe in the crowd, you know?

She also had a crew of kids who raced bicycles and the nerdy geeks in the Girl Scout troop as friends. We used to beat up kids like that, but Emily's gang was different. I'm no dummy: when I saw them face down a teacher who made some crack about being ladylike, I told my crew to leave them alone.

Still, every time I saw her at school, I wanted to do something to wipe that happy smile off her face. I heard that her mother remarried, but if he was anything like Pop, that wouldn't make her so happy all the time. She wasn't a retard, because she was always on the honor roll. Don't you just hate the ones who are smart *and* good-looking?

Seeing her made my stomach roil. My elbow ached, but the doctor said it was in my head. Maybe. *She* sure as hell was in my head, and she wrecked the elbow, even if the doc said it was fine.

***

It happened on a rare warm day in January of our sophomore year. I couldn't wait until next summer, when I'd turn eighteen and quit the stupid school. No one could make me go back then.

But I still wasn't square with Hampstead. I thought of running her off the road, but everyone knows my truck. The cops would have me in no time. Maybe I could catch her coming home at night, but I needed to be at the pizzeria then.

That Saturday, I was driving south on Hesston Road. The cops are all busy on I-135, so it's like a free pass to let the truck run like hell.

Then I saw her up ahead, pedaling down the road alone. *Damn! She's fast.* I wondered if the rest of her racing team rode like that.

I don't know what I was thinking, but a rage made me slide to the right to knock her over.

The tires screamed as the truck hit the curb. I smelled burning rubber just before the truck flew into the air and began rolling. In slow motion, I saw the world turn completely around. The last thing I remembered before my butt and back slammed into the seat was a question:

Where the hell was she?

I woke up lying on a stretcher. Red and blue lights were doing a strobe effect on the side of my truck. A paramedic was pulling my eye open and shouting at me. Well, it *felt* like shouting, but her voice was so distant, I wasn't sure.

Oh, my name.

"William Medford."

"Good, follow my finger." She waved a finger in front of me, and I did as I was told. She was cute in a tough way. Instead of the blue rescue squad uniform, I could imagine jeans and a cowboy hat, or maybe camo, like those girl soldiers. Come to think of it, the girls who ride through Newton on the TransAmerica Trail look like that.

Meanwhile, another paramedic was fastening a brace around my neck.

The world became clearer, and I tried to sit up.

"Not yet, William. We need to check you out in the hospital before you move."

"But—"

"You could have a back or neck injury that you won't feel until you move. Just relax and let us do our job."

And there she was. Emily. Standing with another paramedic on one side and a cop on the other. Everyone else vanished.

"What are you doing here?"

"I called 9-1-1. I'll come see you to tell you what happened."

Then they were lifting me onto a gurney on the road. When that was strapped into the ambulance, the journey to NMC Hospital began. I stared at the ceiling and the gear hanging from the sides of the space in the back. The female paramedic smiled, and she also stroked my face to keep me awake when I wanted to doze off.

"We need you to stay awake until you're checked for concussion."

***

You would think that the first person I would see when I woke up the next morning would be my mother. Instead, I saw Emily Hampstead. My first reaction imploded under a strange feeling of being glad to see her.

"You!"

"Yeah, me. Your mother said I could wait for you to wake up. Otherwise, the staff would not have let me stay."

"Why?"

"You could have been killed, you dummy! What were you thinking?"

"I wasn't – and where the hell did you go?"

"I saw you in my rear-view mirror and jumped on the sidewalk before you hit where I would have been."

"Oh." Somehow that made sense, though I wondered why.

"Well? What were you thinking?"

I didn't know what to say. Suddenly, all my rage and anger and hurt – hell, everything I felt about Emily Hampstead began to melt away. She looked honestly concerned and caring – and pissed at the same time. I know she's younger than me, but it was how Mom looked when she would come to the police station to get me.

"I, I—wasn't. I was just so – I don't know. Angry. Pissed."

She didn't say anything. I'm not one for long silences, no matter how romantic they seem – and this was definitely *not* romantic!

"Why are you here?"

"Trying to sort out whatever it is between us."

"Meaning?"

"Meaning that you've had it in for me ever since seventh grade. And it's getting worse. I can read it on your face every time I see you at school. You were just a bully back then. I read some books about bullies in the library, and you aren't one anymore. At least, you don't act like one."

"What makes you so smart anyway?"

"I'm no smarter than you, but I did talk to my mother about this, in addition to what I read. I don't think you realize how smart you are. And you're a natural leader. I've learned a thing or two about leadership in Girl Scouts, and you have it in spades."

"That sounds like garbage to me. What do you want?"

"Nothing for me. But it makes me sad to see you so angry. You're not my favorite person, William Medford, but I don't hate you. Why do you hate me?"

"Because you broke my arm."

"I did not. It hurt, but it cleared up as soon as they put your joint back, didn't it?"

"And you got me thrown out of school. Do you have any idea what it's like to have your mother be your teacher?"

"I do, actually, because she *is* a teacher, but I didn't get you thrown out. In fact, my mother persuaded the principal *not* to take action on the bus incident. You got yourself thrown out for picking on kids at recess."

She arched an eyebrow as if daring me to contradict her. I took a breath, but then let it out.

"I'm sorry, Emily. I don't get all this."

"I'm sorry too, but I'm glad you're not badly hurt. The doctor said they want to run some X-rays to make sure nothing was cracked, but then they'll release you. And your truck is okay. I called Mr. Curtis. He towed it to his shop and called me this morning. Something about leaks in the shocks from the impact, but you can fix them yourself."

"Yeah, I know how to do that. Thanks."

"You're welcome." She stood and walked to the bed. "Get well quick. I want to watch you change those shocks. Mr. Curtis said we can do it in shop. Then it won't cost you anything."

She squeezed my hand, smiled, and let herself out.

I still hate that girl, but, dammit, it sure is hard.

The Prom

THE DOOR TO THE MUDROOM SQUEAKED. Emily put a pencil in her French textbook and stood as Katherine stopped at the kitchen door to take off her bike shoes. Emily went to the sink.

"How was your day?" She handed Katherine a tall glass of water. The older woman chugged it down before answering.

"Fine. In addition to all the classes going smoothly, no one came to office hours."

"That's unusual, isn't it?"

"For me, yes. I was able to finish reviewing the book on the history of American military nursing and send it to the editor."

"That's great! You've been working on that since we came to Newton."

"Longer than that, if you count all the research and brainstorming before I started writing."

"So, we'll soon have a best seller on the shelves?"

"Hardly. University of Chicago is an academic press. I figure the editor, you, and Mark will be my only readers. Maybe a couple of students trying for brownie points."

"I'm glad you let me read the manuscript. I liked it."

"Thanks, dear. And how was your day?"

"Easy. We had a study hall, so I got all my homework done." She waved at the kitchen table. "I'm reading ahead in French. A short story about a girl cycling in the Loire Valley."

Katherine took a protein shake from the refrigerator. "Did you get my note about supper?"

"Yes. The casserole's thawed, but it's too early to put it in the oven. I didn't expect you home so soon."

"Southerly winds today – in case the sweat didn't tell you."

"Mark should be back in plenty of time."

"Good. Thanks for your help, Emily. I want to remember to say that often, especially now that there is an extra mouth to feed."

"He does like to take us out, you know."

Katherine rinsed out the protein shake bottle. "You finish your story. I'll go shower and change."

"Don't forget your stretches." Emily winked and grinned. Her mother sometimes forgot to stretch, which could lead to cramped muscles.

***

Mark took a second helping of casserole and topped off everyone's wine glass.

"You look pensive all of a sudden, Emily."

"Just thinking." She sighed. "The junior prom is next month."

"No one has asked you?"

"No." She shrugged. "And I don't expect anyone to."

"I noticed that you've never brought anyone home. Any reason for that?"

Emily and Katherine exchanged glances. Mark had been Emily's stepfather for only three years, but she had adored him since before he proposed to Katherine. Still, he often seemed surprised by the experiences his new wife and stepdaughter had shared before they met him.

"I'm not exactly Miss Popularity at school. Most of the kids are friendly enough, but I run with two crowds that don't attract boys: a Girl Scout troop that does wild camping and a road racing team. Neither of those involves the school."

"And you're an honor roll student," said Katherine. "All in all, you must be intimidating, dear."

"I was going to say awesome," said Mark. Emily smiled.

"Nice of you to say, but my escort is expected to be unrelated, and, ideally, matriculated at my educational institution." She affected a British public-school accent. They chuckled.

"You really want to go to the prom, don't you?" said Mark.

"Not for its own sake, I think. I like dancing, and I enjoyed the other dances. But the prom is different. It means so much to my friends, and I want to see them having a good time. I'm the only one who doesn't have a boyfriend or at least a date for the prom."

Katherine looked over her wine glass at the conversation. Emily recognized that look and braced herself for something surprising.

"Why are you waiting for someone to ask?"

"Huh?"

"You could ask someone you like."

"All my friends are girls, Mom. You know I'm not lesbian or anything. We already have two gay couples coming."

"It's the twenty-first century. No one needs to know who asked whom."

Mark said. "I remember being in awe of the smart girls who played varsity. If I were your age at Newton High, I would dream of taking you to the prom, but I'd be too scared to ask."

"So, find some shy guy hiding in the library?"

"Or bring one of the road racers who's not at your school or is home-schooled."

Emily took a sip of her wine. She smiled at them. "I was thinking of going by myself, but finding a date could be fun. Thanks."

***

"Hey, Antoine," Emily said to the back of the student three lockers down from hers. She had admired that broad back and those muscular legs often enough in the peloton with the K-bikes team. Problem was that he always rode off immediately after each ride, so she never had a chance to chat with him. They were the only riders who showed up on their bicycles rather than with the bikes on a car.

Antoine straightened and jumped.

"Jeez, Em. You scared the shit outta me!"

"Sorry. I didn't know you were concentrating."

"Not that. It's just that you move so quietly."

"Oh. Well, sorry again. I have something to ask you, but not here." She looked at the hallway teeming with shouting students rushing to their classes. He fell in next to her as they walked to math. "I noticed you started riding to school this year. Do you live nearby?"

"Close enough. Anderson Avenue. I would rather ride than take the bus."

"I totally understand that."

"You've never taken the bus, have you?"

"Not since seventh grade."

"It took until last summer and some help from Matt to convince my mother to let me ride. I so prefer this." Matt Owens was the owner of K-bikes and the team coach.

"Would you let me ride with you today? Maybe get an ice cream or coffee at Dillon's?"

"I guess." Antoine looked around. No one was paying attention. He gave her a quick grin. "I couldn't drop you if you wanted to follow me. See you at the bike rack."

They found their seats just as the bell rang.

***

Antoine and Emily carried their sundaes to the table in the corner. Emily almost tripped when he pulled out her chair and held it for her.

"No one's ever done that for me."

"My mama taught me to hold doors, and to offer my seat on the bus, too."

"Well, *my* mama's not much for what she calls sexist gallantry. It took my stepfather a whole year to get her to stop complaining when he would open the car door for her." She smiled. "One day he said that he doesn't act that way for bitches and phonies, so she would have to stop being a lady if she wanted him to stop being a gentleman – or something like that."

He laughed as he sat. They each spooned a bite of their ice cream, while he looked intently at her.

"What do you want to talk about, Em?"

"Have you asked anyone to the prom?" Antoine dropped his spoon. He took a napkin to wipe up the spilled ice cream on the table.

"Are you kidding?"

"No. Mary and Joanna are going, and my two friends in the scout troop. I'd like to go too."

"Are you asking me?"

"Sure. Do you have a date already?"

"Of course not. I wasn't going."

"Why not? It's the prom."

Antoine stretched out his arm alongside Emily's. "You even have to ask why?"

Emily stared at the shining limb next to hers. The muscles in his forearm rippled as he tapped his middle finger. It looked familiar.

"Do you play piano?"

Antoine dropped his jaw.

"Yes. How did you know?"

"The way the muscles in your arm move when you tap your finger."

He pulled his jaw back in position. "What's that got to do with – wait a minute! Is that the first thing you just noticed about my arm?"

"Well, yeah. And how shiny your skin is. It's cool."

Antoine took his arm back. "Emily, you are one weird girl. You didn't just notice what color my skin is?"

"Sure, after I noticed your arm muscles. They're much more interesting."

"You're putting me on, right?"

"No. Why would you think that?"

"Because this is America, and I'm Black. The only one in our class, I might add."

"So? We're friends; we're on the same racing team – and both on the honor roll, *I might add.*"

"Because this is Newton, population less than twenty thousand and ninety-percent white."

They ate their sundaes in silence. When they were almost finished, Emily asked, "I know almost nothing about you, because you always ride off alone. I know you came for freshman year. Where were you before?"

"Fort Hood, Texas. You?"

"Fredericksburg, Virginia. We came here in time for seventh grade."

"I'd expect a Southern belle to understand race relations better than you seem to."

"Tell me about your family, and I'll tell you about mine. Then maybe we'll each understand better."

"What do you want to know?"

"What brought you here. What your family does. What you like or hate – that sort of thing." She put down her spoon. "For example, my mother teaches at Wichita State. Feminist literature. She moved here from a better-paying job at Mary Washington University after my father was killed. We were pretty much basket cases after that until she met my stepfather, Mark. They were married three years ago. You?"

"Mine retired from the Army. She was an instructor at the Nurse Corps School in Fort Hood. Dad was killed in Afghanistan. My grandparents live here, and they're not well. Mom is an ER nurse at Newton Medical Center. No stepfather. I wish."

"Do you miss Texas?"

"Not really. I don't have any friends outside our church, but at least I don't get the unsolicited hatred I got there. And I do have my family."

They stared for a while. He dropped his gaze first.

"Are you afraid to go to prom?"

"No. Well, yes. Probably nothing at the prom itself, but I would worry about the bullying later and the things that could happen."

"Such as?"

"I've already come back to my bike to find it vandalized. Usually, a red N painted on the saddle. Three times since the shootings last year. I worry about slashed tires or loosened bolts if someone wants to teach me a lesson." He held his hands up and made air quotes.

Emily did not hide her astonishment. "I'm sorry, Antoine, but that's bullshit!"

"Yeah, but it happens."

Emily sat and thought. Antoine picked up their empty dishes and took them to the recycling bin.

"I want to think about this. If you don't go with me, you won't go?"

"Of course not."

"Don't ask anyone else until I get back to you, then."

He laughed. "You got some guts, Em. I'm looking forward to the ride tomorrow after school."

***

When the K-bikes team rolled into the Newton High School parking lot, the sun was still up. The racers hefted their bicycles onto the various cars and vans. Antoine rode to the street without saying anything.

"Not so fast, Dewberry, " Emily shouted at him. "Wait for me."

She made the left turn into traffic on Twelfth Street with him. The other teenage riders stopped and stared at the pair riding away. Some of them had never noticed Antoine except during the rides; they could not have told you how he got there or how he left after each ride.

"Can I come home with you, today or soon?"

"You're kidding."

"No. I want to meet your mother. She must be awesome, running an emergency room, and taking care of aging parents and you, by herself."

"Em, you know what happens to Black boys who are seen hanging with white girls?"

"Antoine, this is Kansas, not Mississippi."

"You'd be surprised."

They rode for a couple of blocks.

"Well, do you have time to meet my mom?"

"Mama is on second shift today, but—"

"Good. Let's go to my place. Just to meet her. Follow me."

He sighed. "I usually follow you, Em. So does everyone else on the team."

***

"Mom, this is Antoine Dewberry. He's in my class."

"And on the K-bikes team, I see." Katherine wiped her hands on her apron and shook hands with the boy in the racing team kit.

"Please to meet you, Mrs. Hampstead."

"It's Dempsey now, but I'm still getting used to it myself."

"Oh, yeah. Emily told me."

"I asked Antoine about the prom, and he's trying to educate me on the realities of race relations in America. Can we talk about this?"

"Emily, let's meet him first, shall we?" She took off her apron. "Something to drink, Antoine? If you just came off the training ride, you'll want both water and a protein shake."

"Thank you, ma'am."

"Emily?" She signaled with her head for Emily to serve the drinks. "Come, Antoine, let's sit in the living room."

Emily brought the tray out. Katherine and Antoine had just sat down.

"Your mother is Major Yvette Dewberry, isn't she?"

Antoine did not contain his surprise. "Yes, ma'am. How did you know?"

"It's an uncommon surname. I interviewed her last year for a book I was writing. She's quite a hero in the nursing community. You didn't know?"

"Well, she has a bunch of medals, but she doesn't like to talk about what she did."

"I know what you mean. It took me a long time to get her to open up."

Antoine shook his head. "I never would have expected that. You probably know more about her than I do."

"I don't think so. We just know different things. She isn't my mother after all. And you're a third-generation Army brat. Both your grandparents were in Vietnam, weren't they?"

"I'm not sure. I just know that they're old."

"Your grandparents look older than they should because they were both exposed to Agent Orange. I wrote a whole chapter on nurses in Southeast Asia, and your grandmother figured in it."

"Mom, I want to meet his family, even if he won't go to the prom with me."

"Well, now that I know that Yvette and her mother are in town, I'd like to see them again. Antoine, would you mind if we gave her a call?"

"No. Not at all, ma'am." He dictated their home phone number. "I'm stunned."

He was still shaking his head as he rode down their driveway, his lights blinking in the failing daylight. Mark pulled his Tesla well to the right to give him plenty of room.

***

"Hey, Em." Emily jumped, spilling her physics book.

"You're pretty sneaky yourself, Antoine." She picked up the book and closed the locker. "What's up?"

"Come home with me. I want to talk to my mama about the prom, and I want you there."

Emily glanced around. "You're sure?" Since Antoine had mentioned the shootings in February of last year, she was more aware of the sour looks on some of the students.

"Yes. She wants to meet the daughter of the professor who convinced her to talk about her time on active duty. Before your mother comes."

"Oh, okay, I guess."

They walked out to their bikes. Their houses were less than five hundred yards apart as the crow flies, and less than a mile from school off Twelfth Street.

After they leaned their bikes inside the garage, Antoine's mother came through the mudroom. A trim woman with no gray in her short hair, her physique and her height explained Antoine's athletic appearance. She had crow's feet when she smiled, which must be often. When the smile relaxed, Emily noticed the set of a jaw in a face that exacted unquestioning obedience. *Not like a mother,* she thought. *A commander.*

"So, this is the famous Emily Hampstead. Come in!" She held the door for them. "Antoine has issues of *Cycling News* all over the house. You're in the last two."

"Pleased to meet you, Ms. Dewberry. Those articles were a surprise. Who would care about a mid-level race in Kansas?"

"No one would notice a small bike shop team taking all three places on the podium at the Midwest Regionals? C'mon!" She opened the refrigerator. "Something to drink?"

When they were seated in the living room with pineapple juice, Ms. Dewberry said, "I know you have to get home, so I'll be direct. Why did you ask Antoine to the prom?"

"I wanted to go, and he's the only guy friend I have at school."

"You're a beautiful girl, Emily. Why no friends?"

"Thank you, ma'am. I didn't say no friends, just no male friends. The guys I hang out with are at K-bikes or on the racing team, and Antoine is the only one of those at school with me."

"You like older men, I take it." She grinned as she said it. Antoine looked down; he would have blushed if he could.

"Not especially. But Antoine smiled at me when he showed up for his first training ride freshman year."

"She'd been riding with them unofficially for two years already," said Antoine. "Even then, she was the fastest rider on the team." He looked at Emily. "And to be fair, you smiled first. No one else looked like they wanted me there."

"Matt took a gamble on me as a twelve-year-old girl. No surprise that he was more interested in the way you ride than anything else."

Yvette had been switching her gaze back and forth during this exchange. "Which brings us to the crux of the matter. Why would you invite a boy to the prom? And a Black boy at that?"

"Because who cares who invites whom? As my mother pointed out when the prom came up at supper, this is the twenty-first century. We're on the same team, but we're both nerds at school, because cycling isn't football. We're both on the honor roll, and I noticed that he checks out the same books at the library that I do.

"It doesn't hurt that he's smoking hot." She grinned at Antoine's stunned look. "C'mon, Antoine, hasn't anyone ever whistled at you?"

Yvette laughed. A pleasant, musical laugh. "Girl, you are a piece of work!"

"I'll take that as a compliment, ma'am."

"It is. Now, haven't you thought about the fact that he is Black and you're not?"

"Honestly, until he mentioned it, no." She glanced at Antoine and back at Yvette. "Should I?"

"Our reality, Emily, is that almost everyone does — and first. On top of that, Larry Ford's girlfriend was white. The shootings at the Excel plant have everyone noticing mixed-race couples more than they would have."

"Well, almost everyone I meet assumes that a girl can't race or run or defend herself. It makes me push back."

"Not the same. I'm a woman, too, so I understand what you mean, but race complicates everything in America."

They sipped their juice in silence.

Emily said, "I've read about white privilege, so I know this could backfire on Antoine worse than on me. But it makes me mad. I like you, Antoine. This is just not fair." She looked at his mother. "Any ideas?"

"Actually, yes, but now that I've met you and formed an impression, it's time for me to meet your mother again – and your stepfather. I am pleased that you take after her the way I expected."

"She wants to see you again, too."

"Antoine told me, and she called this afternoon. We agreed to meet tomorrow afternoon. You don't have another date, do you?" She chuckled and stood.

"No, ma'am." Emily and Antoine stood. "It was a pleasure to meet you."

They walked to the garage. Antoine opened the door while Emily donned her helmet. The sun was still up, but she turned on her blinking lights anyway.

***

"It's as close to a limo as I can get, Antoine. Hop in."

"Where's Emily, Mr. Dempsey?" Antoine climbed in the back of the Tesla and closed the door.

"At home. She may have invited you, but I'm old fashioned enough to make the gentleman go pick up his date. Your mothers should be at the school by now."

"I didn't expect my mama to volunteer to be a chaperone. She hasn't been active with the school."

"Most working single moms can't. It's the same with Emily's mother. But I think it's brilliant. Either one of them could quell a riot. Together, they'll be like a SWAT team before anything happens."

"Yeah, I guess. Mama can be pretty scary."

Mark pulled up outside the Dempsey home. Emily came out in a fetching gown that flared enough below the hips for her legs to move freely. The sleeveless top showed off her well-toned muscles, which made observers notice her shoulders and head before her chest. Her hair was done up in a sort of reverse French braid. At least that's what she called it.

Antoine and Mark both stared until Mark said, "Stunning, Emily."

"Yeah, you look great."

"Thanks, both of you. It feels weird. I don't think I've worn anything more formal than a skirt and blouse since the wedding."

Antoine held the car door for her. "First time for everything. Mama had to show me how to put on this tux." Inside the car, he slipped a corsage on her wrist.

A few minutes later, Mark eased up behind someone's rented limousine outside the school. Antoine leaped out and went around to hand Emily out of the car.

"Call me when you're ready to go. I may sneak in myself, but don't you think about that."

"Thank you, Mr. Dempsey."

He started to move, then stopped the car. "And remember what I said, driver service includes any post-prom parties that you might want to attend. I'm just the chauffer tonight, seriously."

"Thanks, Mark." Emily bent her knees and waved at him.

Antoine held out his arm. Emily took it and they walked smoothly past the couples who paused to stare, outside the school and down the hall.

***

Katherine put down her book when she heard the parking brake of the Tesla in the garage. She came downstairs in her bathrobe just as Mark and Emily walked into the kitchen.

"Mom, you didn't have to stay up for us."

"I know. I only got back an hour ago. Yvette and I had drinks at her house before I came home. You two looked like you were having a very good time. Want to tell me about the post-prom shenanigans or wait until breakfast?"

"I'd love to stay up. This was such a wonderful night that I don't want it to end. But we do have church tomorrow."

"Breakfast, then." Katherine kissed her daughter before she headed up the stairs. "Good night, dear."

Mark took Katherine in his arms and kissed her, long and passionately.

"And how was your driving gig, dear?"

"I had fun, too. Apart from the fact that I could stream books or movies in the car, I really enjoyed watching the kids. They had a ball at the prom, and even more fun at the pizza joint and Joanna's house."

"They can party hard, can't they? It's four a.m."

"Oh, to be a teenager again."

"Not me. Not for anything. Twenty-five maybe, but not a teenager." She hugged him. "C'mon, let's have our own post-prom party." She loosened his tie and led him upstairs with it....

Adieu, Antoine

EMILY TURNED INTO THE PARKING LOT outside Newton High School and circled six laps while the rest of the K-Bikes team followed her in. They gathered at the end where almost all the riders had cars waiting to take them home.

Chugging water bottles and flapping their open jerseys, they tried to cool down until the coach arrived in the broom car. A high-pressure dome had trapped hot, wet air over Kansas and Nebraska for two weeks.

"Hey, Em! You were smoking today." Pete gave her a thumbs-up. "You ready for the Air Force Invitational?"

"I don't know. I feel good, but what will it be like at seven thousand feet?"

Matt Owens, the coach, got out of the car. "We'll find out soon enough." He waved in a circle. "Gather round."

Emily straddled her bike next to Antoine, giving him a friendly nudge. He smiled. They focused on the coach.

"Well done today, everyone," said Matt. "I've got some good news and some bad news. The good news is that four of you qualified for the Air Force Academy Invitational: Emily, Anna, Samira, and Judy." Emily was the youngest, a rising high school senior. Anna worked at

K-bikes; Samira and Judy attended Bethel College. "That's not enough for a team, but I've arranged with my friend in Denver to combine our riders with theirs. They have eight qualifiers, which gives us a dozen – enough for a solid peloton.

"The van will seat eight, so any of you who want to come as support, let me know. Also, please get your release forms back – Emily, I have yours."

"What's the bad news, Coach?" asked Pete.

"The bad news is that Antoine is leaving us."

While the team surrounded the tall Black rider with shouts of dismay, Emily held in her sorrow. Antoine had told her quickly before the ride and promised to explain afterward. They usually rode to Dillon's together before going home, so she bided her time at the edge of the crowd.

"Saturday's a training day," said the coach. "We'll start focusing on the Air Force race, so I only need the women here. The men are welcome to tag along for the workout – and it will be a workout, I promise."

The other riders heaved bikes onto their cars, while Emily and Antoine rode away, turning left to go east on Twelfth Street.

"Come home with me, would you?" Antoine said. "I don't feel like Dillon's today." Emily glanced quickly at his troubled face.

"Okay with me. I don't think I want to discuss this in public either."

They turned onto Anderson Avenue and parked their bikes in the garage of the home just past Eleventh Street, which had sheltered his mother's family for two generations. Antoine's maternal grandparents no longer lived there. His grandfather had died last year, and his grandmother was in hospice care near the Newton Medical Center.

"My mama will be back soon," Antoine said as he pulled a couple of protein shakes from the refrigerator. Emily set her shake on the table and put her arms around him.

"There is no way I'm going to feel good about this so just hug me first."

After a minute, they shared a long passionate kiss. Only the knowledge that Major Yvette Dewberry, Nurse Corps, US Army (retired) would walk in soon kept them from going further.

"Tell me." Emily sat at the kitchen table and swallowed some protein drink.

"Mama and I only decided on this yesterday. She sent an email to Grandpop last night. He answered this afternoon, and she texted me on my way to the ride." He paused for a drink. "You know I want to go to UVA after we graduate, right?"

"Well, that, but also William and Mary, Virginia Tech, and James Madison University, if I recall correctly. Oh, and Shenandoah University for piano."

"All in Virginia." He took a deep breath. "Grandpop and Mariah said I can live with them for senior year and apply as a state resident."

"Aren't they on the Eastern Shore somewhere?"

"Wallops Island, where Grandpop used to work. I spent summers there when Dad was alive." Emily's felt a tug in her chest when she saw his gaze go distant. Antoine's father died in Afghanistan when he was eleven. Having lost her father in second grade, thinking of his dad always brought back that terrible day to Emily. "It makes such a big difference in tuition that we'd be crazy to pass on the opportunity."

"Couldn't you just claim their address?"

"We talked about that, but not knowing who would invite me for tours or interviews, it makes sense to be closer than Kansas."

Emily wanted to cry, and she clenched her hands under the table. She had told herself too many times that it was puppy love, a silly crush, etc., etc., but nothing worked. Except for Mark, her stepfather, Antoine was the first male she had ever wanted to get close to. He was intelligent, gentle, strong, and wise beyond his years. She knew that he felt as strongly for her as she did for him.

She forced herself to keep a straight face, because – strange as it seemed – she also felt happy for her friend. They had talked for hours about the future, and their hopes looking beyond their last year at Newton High School. She had thought of applying to UVA herself, but she had too many variables in play to focus on college selection yet. After all, Virginia held painful memories for her.

"I thought we'd be living in Virginia, too, until—" He nodded as she paused. "What about your mother and grandmother here?"

"Mama will stay. This is the home she grew up in. Grannie may die soon, but Mama doesn't need to be with me in Virginia."

"I'm going to miss you terribly."

"And I'll miss you."

"The Eastern Shore is flatter than Kansas. You'll never get in shape."

He laughed and shrugged. She finished her protein shake and went to the sink to rinse out the bottle.

"School starts here next week. What about there?"

"Wednesday after Labor Day. Mama and I leave next Thursday."

"Oh!" She could not keep the disappointment from her voice. "So soon."

They heard the garage door opening and went to greet his mother.

***

Katherine put the lesson plans and other papers in her pannier, checked around the desk, and turned off the light in her office. Passing her daughter's room, she heard a sound she had not heard in years. She knocked on the door gently.

"Emily, may I come in?" The muffled grunt sounded affirmative, so she opened the door. Emily lay on her bed fully clothed, sobbing into her pillow. "What wrong, honey?"

"He only left this morning, and I already miss him so much! I don't even know if I'll ever see him again." The girl swung upright and sat on her bed. Katherine sat with her and put her arm around her daughter's shoulders. Emily leaned into her chest. "I couldn't even say goodbye because we had school."

They sat there for a while, Katherine squeezing her shoulder, and Emily crying herself out.

"Don't you have his email and home address?"

"Yes, but what if he never writes back?"

Katherine thought, *why did she have to be such an introvert? I guess in the long run, it's better than a party girl getting in trouble.*

"I wouldn't think about that now, sweetie. He hasn't even arrived in Virginia yet." She shook the arm wrapped around Emily. "He is not the only boy around, you know."

"But every time I dance or hang out with other guys, I'm always comparing them to Antoine."

"He is exceptional, I know. Before you met him, you seemed to have a good time with your friends. You can do that again. And before you know it, you'll both be leaving for college."

"But that's a whole year away."

"True, but you can try to stay in touch. I'm sure if anything earth-shattering happens, Yvette will let me know."

"I'm glad you two are friends."

"Me, too." She reached for a tissue and handed it to Emily. "Feeling better yet?"

"No, but there isn't anything I can do about my feelings."

"True. Recognizing them as feelings is good. You'll both get past this."

"I don't *want* to get over him."

"I said 'get past this,' not 'get over him.' This is an event in both your lives. Let's see what lies ahead, eh?"

"I guess." Emily blew her nose and tossed the tissue in the waste basket. "Thanks, Mom. I think I'll go to bed now." She stood and started undressing. Katherine went to the door.

"Good night, dear."

"Good night, Mom."

Mark closed his book and looked up as Katherine came in, taking out her earrings. When she came back from the bathroom, he pulled the covers down for her.

"How is our broken heart? I figured you didn't need me."

"No. Thanks for not coming in. She needed to cry it out."

"Everything is so intense at that age."

"Like I said after the prom, I would never want to be a teenager again."

"She didn't have any boyfriends before, so it's a double whammy for her, isn't it?"

"Kind of. Apart from the fact he's her first crush, most of the boys she meets don't impress her. Antoine was everything they weren't. Too late to have her go to a private school or move to a big city, isn't it?"

"We could move to Wichita, but I wouldn't rip her from Newton after all the energy she's expended getting accepted and coming into her own here. She's a hero to her friends. I think she'll survive the lack of romance long enough to go away to college."

"For a man who never had kids, you sure are smart, you know?" She pushed his book aside and rolled onto him....

Pay It Forward

(from the novel, *Emily & Hilda*)

EMILY SCREAMED. Her eardrums exploded as intense white light surrounded her. She felt herself falling to the left as the bicycle flew out from under her. She tucked and landed on her hip and shoulder.

Blinded and hearing nothing but ringing in her ears, she smelled ozone. The earth felt damp beneath her, cooling the road rash on her side and shoulder. A buzzing sensation on the back of her neck and over her head seemed to push against her helmet.

She felt the pain build in her shoulder and left arm. The darkness after the white light resolved into swirling colors and shapes as her vision returned. Out here in the middle of nowhere, there was nothing to hear, but she thought the ringing was less.

After a few minutes, she blinked and looked around. Her bicycle lay against the bottom of a blackened and smoking oak tree, planted by a farming family long gone. Steam mingled with the smoke from the wet stump. Bits of branches, bark, and wood lay on the ground downwind from the tree.

She got up carefully. Trying to hug herself hurt her arm even worse. The rain that had soaked her had stopped, but the wind was picking up. That rain had also soaked the oak leaves littering the road and caused her crash.

She regretted going out on this training ride alone. Mary and Joanna had both backed out at the last minute. Emily was at least twenty miles from town, and it would be dark in another hour and a half.

She worried about her arm, but she was sure that it was only scraped badly and not broken. Still, her favorite Shebeest bicycle jersey was bloodstained and torn, and her spandex shorts had big holes on the left side. The road rash on her arm and side and the cut on her cheek were clotting.

She was more worried about her bicycle, a three-thousand-dollar Colnago that her stepfather had bought for her birthday four months ago. She had been winning amateur racing events all season and was hoping to win two more races before winter consigned her to the spinning studio at the gym until spring. She shivered and walked over to the bike.

The front wheel looked like a pretzel after hitting the tree when she flew off the pavement on her left side. Lifting it up, she tried to roll it, but the front wheel ran into the fork, and the bike stopped. Her mood shifted from tears to frustration.

It occurred to her that not having a little tool kit under her saddle was probably a bigger oversight than taking the risk of riding alone. She shrugged; she didn't know how to fix anything anyway.

She reached for her cell phone and found the whole pocket missing from her jersey. The cell phone was lying in two pieces on the pavement where she had fallen. She pocketed the pieces and picked up the bike.

At least the Colnago was light. She hefted it on her good shoulder and started walking along the highway. She was hardly an elegant sight, wobbling awkwardly in her cleated, hard plastic racing shoes. She considered going in her socks, but the gravel on the edge of the road was sharp and nasty looking.

With something to do – even if unpleasant – she felt her scrapes less, except maybe for the bruise on her left hip, which was her main shock absorber hitting the pavement. She figured that, at worst, she could make it back to town in three hours, if she could not hitch a ride.

Hitchhiking. Her mother would have a bigger fit over that idea than her riding alone. The lack of any traffic was the main reason that she trained on this highway, which ran to an abandoned army post fifty miles west of town. Her parents would be at the Durstens' party until after midnight, so no one would miss her as she hiked along the deserted road.

After a half hour, she had stopped shivering. She took off her shoes, tied them to the saddle post, and started walking on the pavement. It was not comfortable, but she was moving at a better clip. The bicycle, light as it was, had begun to dig into her shoulder, so the smoother gait helped with that.

Cornfields extended in all directions as the asphalt ribbon seemed to disappear into a yellow tunnel of corn in the distance. She had never really looked at the scenery – or lack of it – before. As the shadows from the stalks spread across the road, she noticed how the fields went from yellow to golden to purple. As the sun began to sink out of sight behind her, the purple fields slowly turned dark. There were still maybe forty-five minutes of light left.

Emily noticed the Evening Star (Venus, she remembered) appear up ahead while there was still plenty of light. Beyond the rustle of the wind, she heard a sound behind her. She shifted as she walked and saw what looked like a small bear with a flashlight in its mouth, weaving back and forth on the road, maybe a quarter mile back. She stopped and squinted.

A bicycle. With panniers. And a dark form sitting almost erect on it.

Emily stared as the bicycle came closer. Bicycle tourists belonged to a different universe, especially the bike-packing variety who often rode through town. Generally unkempt, looking unwashed, with assorted collections of gear lashed to their bicycles and panniers, more like peasants fleeing an invading army than regular people. "As likely to steal supper as buy it," her friends would say, crossing the street to avoid meeting them. The men never shaved, and the women never had their hair combed. Still, Emily wondered why they always seemed so cheerful, why they always waved when her racing team blew past them.

The sound she heard took form. The bicyclist was singing loudly. She weaved happily as if waltzing to the music, which indeed she was. It wasn't a familiar song, and Emily thought that she had all the hits on her playlists.

It *was* a waltz! The rider was not wearing earbuds but was singing from memory—in German. As the rider approached, Emily could see that she was a strong, Black woman. Certainly not a kid, she could be any age from twenty-five to sixty. She was riding a fifty-nine-centimeter frame, which could take a six-foot man. Under her helmet, a smile spread across her face. As she reached the final line of the waltz, the rider leaned back erect and belted out the coda with her arms spread out. Emily guessed that she was rolling at fifteen miles per hour with no hands and four panniers! She grabbed her handlebars and coasted to a stop alongside the stunned Emily. The muscles in her forearms rippled as she braked.

"You know, you got it backwards, girl. It's supposed to carry you, not the other way around." The way she grinned, Emily felt comforted, not put down.

"I crashed, and I'm walking home."

"The next town, I take it."

"Yes. About fifteen miles, I guess."

"Hoo-ey. That's a long hike." She dismounted the bicycle and parked it, supported by a kickstand that would hold up a truck. She smoothly unbuckled and removed her helmet, which she pulled off a long ponytail of shiny black hair. With her angular cheekbones and tall, spare frame, she made Emily think of something awe-inspiring. An Amazon, perhaps.

"Your parents probably don't want you talking to strangers." She put out her hand. "I'm Hilda."

"Emily." She took Hilda's hand and felt her strong, confident grip. She also noticed her crisp, clear accent like the British actors on BBC mysteries. "What brings you here? There's nothing but an abandoned base on that road."

"I know. Which makes it perfect for unmolested camping. The parade ground made a beautiful campsite. The grills in the picnic areas beat campfires any day, and the water still runs in the toilets. Someone forgot to turn that off, I guess."

"Are you crossing the country like the other bicycle tourists I've seen?"

"Probably. If I am, I'm only halfway there, and who knows what will happen tomorrow?"

"But you're alone!"

"So it would seem. And it would seem that so are you."

"But I live here —up there a ways, anyway." Emily looked to the distant end of the road.

"I assume you aren't walking because you like to carry expensive bicycles in the dark."

"Front wheel hit a tree when I slid off the road. Did you see the leaves back where the oak tree is?"

"I did. Went through there shortly after the rain stopped. I hate leaves. They're worse than snow." Hilda pointed to the bike on Emily's shoulder. "What have you got there? May I look?"

Emily swung the bike off her shoulder. Hilda grabbed it easily, flipped it upside down with one hand, and set it gently on its handlebars and seat.

"Very nice bike. You wouldn't have a spoke wrench, would you?"

"I don't have any tools," Emily said apologetically. "If I did, I wouldn't know what to do with them."

"Probably on one of those sponsored teams with a pro wrench to fix everything."

Emily nodded.

"Long-haul touring bikes usually don't break down *except* in places like this. Maybe I can help."

Hilda considered the front wheel. She went to her bicycle, rooted in the right pannier, and came back with a camping lantern, a flashlight, and a zippered bag.

"Got what you need right here. That wheel may look like a pretzel, but it's perfectly formed for the kind of twist the spokes will give the rim if it's hit just right. The rim isn't broken or cracked." She turned on the lantern. "What the hell, girl. You're a mess!"

"It almost doesn't hurt already."

"But that road rash could get infected. Here, you hold the lantern, so we can see this. I'll be right back."

Hilda went back to her pannier and extracted a first aid kit and a pack of disposable wipes, the large kind that hospitals use to bathe patients.

"Ouch!"

"Sorry, but we need to clean this off. Did you see the bits of asphalt and gravel in your wounds?"

"Is that what it was? I was going to clean up when I got home."

"Too much torn flesh to wait for that. Hold still."

Emily winced a few more times as Hilda cleaned out the wounds and applied second skin to the worst of them. "Your face looks okay, now that it's cleaned off. Just let it heal as is."

With her wounds dressed, Emily felt much better already. Hilda put away her first aid kit and came back.

"Let's look at your steed. Hold that lantern up, and I'll show you what to do."

"Thanks." Emily raised the lantern and watched as Hilda loosened the brake and quick-release lever and removed the wheel.

"This is all we need." Hilda held out a steel ring with square cuts in it. "Spoke wrench. They come in different sizes and only weigh a few grams. This one can handle the three most common spoke nipples. Watch."

She set the wheel on the ground and let some air out of the tire. Then she inserted a square cut around a spoke nipple near the valve and twisted it a quarter turn.

"The spoke nipple is a nut on the threaded end of the spoke, right?"

Emily nodded, although this was news to her.

"Think 'righty-tighty, lefty-loosey.' Can you remember that?"

"Righty-tighty, lefty-loosey. Got it."

"That applies to all right-handed screw threads. On your bicycle, that means every thread *except* your left pedal."

Emily nodded again.

"Here's the catch. Think of where the nut goes on the bolt or, in this case, the threaded end of the spoke. We're looking at the wheel from inside the rim, but the spoke nipple is screwed on the *end* of the spoke, so you look at it from the tire side, not the inside. Make sense?"

"Yes." *This is interesting*, Emily thought.

"So, we loosen the spoke this way. See?"

"It looks backwards from here, but not if I imagine looking through the tire."

"Good. Only loosen a quarter or a half turn at a time, so the pressure comes off the wheel evenly as we work our way around. I like to go to the opposite side of the wheel for each next spoke, but some mechanics just work all the way around. I'm playing it safe here. I got the first six. You try some."

Emily gave Hilda the lantern, then worked her way back and forth around the wheel, loosening spokes a little at a time. Suddenly the wheel jumped out of her hands with a twang.

"Omigod! What was that?"

"The wheel righting itself. Are you okay?"

"Just surprised. What about the wheel?"

"It's probably fine. We managed to loosen it all the way without setting anything wrong permanently. Now we just need to tighten and true it."

"You mean, I can ride it?"

"Not now, but you won't walk home."

Hilda showed Emily how to start tightening the spokes carefully so that they exerted their pressure on the rim evenly. Eventually, the wheel felt hand tight.

"Let's put it in the wheel truing jig," said Hilda.

"You have one of those?" Emily asked, looking at the loaded panniers.

"No. You do. It's called a fork. Here, slip the wheel back onto the bike."

Hilda had Emily check the rolling direction of the tire and tighten the quick-release levers after the wheel was in its fork.

"Now, spin the wheel and see where it rubs or wobbles out of line. Then tighten the opposite spokes to pull it over, a quarter turn of the spoke nipple each time." The two of them took turns until the wheel was not wobbling. Then Hilda checked the roundness by holding a screwdriver near the rim as it spun to see if it bulged out of a circular path. It was almost perfect. Emily tightened the opposing pairs of spokes needed to pull the rim into round. Hilda pumped up the tire with the long frame pump from her bike.

"I think you can ride home," Hilda said at last. "It's dark. Do you have a light?"

"No." Emily's elation sagged as she considered the empty, dark road. They could not even see the loom of the lights of town from here.

"Here. Let's lash this flashlight to your handlebars. I'll ride on the centerline side in the unlikely event we meet any other vehicles. Besides, that's an emergency roadside job on the wheel. You should get a new wheel before you go out again."

They put their helmets on and set out together. Hilda's 850W Night Rider headlight lit the road comfortably for both of them, riding side by side. Emily told Hilda about her family, her school, and her racing team. She loved riding more than anything. Hilda turned out to be an army brat whose parents met in Germany, where she was born. Her father retired there, and Hilda grew up bilingual as well as bicultural and biracial. "All-American girl, that's me!" she said. She was only riding as far as town to catch the train to Chicago, where a friend would join her for the eastern half of her trek.

An hour later, they coasted to a stop outside Emily's home. Emily untied the flashlight and gave it to Hilda.

"I don't know how to thank you, Hilda. Why don't you stay the night here? I know my folks won't mind."

"I'd love to, Emily, but I already have an e-ticket for the train tonight, and I don't want to miss it."

"But–"

Hilda put her hand on Emily's shoulder and squeezed gently. The hand was warm, strong, and firm.

"It's okay. Just pay it forward. You know what that means?"

"I think. Do someone else a favor?"

"You got it. Give me a hug and go help someone else someday."

After Hilda's brightly flashing taillight disappeared around the corner, Emily realized that she had never gotten her last name or any contact information. She parked her bike in the garage and went upstairs, snagging a protein bar and a carton of orange juice from the kitchen on the way. She took a shower and put her clothes in the trash. She donned a fresh pair of pajamas. Then she fired up her computer and looked up the winter maintenance class schedule at the K-Bikes bicycle shop.

***

(Links to the novels: https://jthine.com/books)